The [illegible]
In Her Genes

James Goodwin

outskirtspress
DENVER, COLORADO

This is a work of fiction. The events and characters described herein are imaginary and are not intended to refer to specific places or living persons. The opinions expressed in this manuscript are solely the opinions of the author and do not represent the opinions or thoughts of the publisher. The author has represented and warranted full ownership and/or legal right to publish all the materials in this book.

The Truth Is In Her Genes

v3.0

Outskirts Press, Inc.
http://www.outskirtspress.com

ISBN: 978-1-4787-7507-2

Outskirts Press and the “OP” logo are trademarks belonging to Outskirts Press, Inc.

PRINTED IN THE UNITED STATES OF AMERICA

Prologue

Pulling the covers over her head and pretending the phone wasn't ringing didn't make it true, as Holly found out. Still hung over from three days of too much partying, drugs, and booze, it was a wonder that she could find her cell phone. Forget reading the screen to see who was calling—at least she knew it was 4:30, according the large digital clock on her bedside table.

"Hello."

Mrs. K spoke quickly but in a clear, strong voice. "Holly, I need you to work tonight"

"What? No way! I worked the Detroit Auto Show last weekend and the political caucus meeting on Tuesday and Wednesday. You told me I wouldn't be scheduled for a few days," complained Holly.

"Holly, it has been a few days. Do you even know the time or day?"

"Yeah, its 4:30 in the morning on Thursday…no, Friday," responded Holly.

"Holly, it's Saturday and it's 4:30 in the afternoon. If you want to continue working at Elite Personal Services, you are going to stop the drugs and drinking. Hell, you look like a burned out 40- year-old instead of a 22-year-old. Let me make it clear if you don't make it to the job tonight, you are through. Now get yourself together and be at the Delta Pi Theta Fraternity at Middle Ohio University on State St. by 9:00. I am already down one girl and I don't want to be short one more." Holly had been to the Delts' house several times for parties when she was in high school, but this was the first time going as a working girl.

It took a while for her eyes to focus on the hovel that was her bedroom. Clothes were thrown haphazardly on the dresser, nightstand and the floor. The room reeked of dirty laundry, stale cigarette butts, and vomit—which thankfully she missed stepping in. She had a lot of work ahead getting herself together if she was going to pull off looking like a sexy co-ed. She couldn't lose this job or she would be working the streets again. This one-bedroom apartment was the nicest place she had ever lived and she wasn't going to screw it up.

Standing in front of the steamy bathroom mirror, Holly saw the results of a life of excessive partying. Her eyes were bloodshot, her sickly pallor induced by her lifestyle, and her hair matted together with who knows what. Thankfully, her body still looked good. The small firm tits and firm butt gave her body the look of an athletic teenager. That was a joke, since the closest she got to being athletic was on the mattress. She was just blessed with good genes when it came to her body.

She never had been close to her parents and wasn't surprised when they kicked her out of their house when she turned eighteen just two months before graduation. The last straw was when their house was spray painted with some pretty nasty words: "The home of Holly, queen of the blow jobs". A time before that someone sprayed on the family car "Holly gives a gift that keeps on giving –STD's. Her parents weren't the worst kind. She was never abused but they made it clear that she was a mistake. They never wanted children and barely tolerated her through the first 18 years so cutting her loose didn't conflict them at all.

It wasn't always like this. Four years ago, when she left high school she thought her future was acting and she was going to be the next Kaley Cuoco. She had the cute figure, girl-next-door looks, and the attitude to go with it. She definitely knew the high school boys liked her and she wasn't afraid to experiment with sex, drugs, or alcohol. At the first keg party she attended, Holly didn't think twice about taking her top off when all the boys gathered around her and started chanting her name. She was the girl every guy wanted to have a piece of, and by the end of the year that almost was the case. She knew all the girls looked down on her, but she just assumed they were jealous.

The film career didn't take off, but she still had hopes. She first responded to an ad in the back of a pulp magazine she bought at the cashier's counter at Kroger's. The ad simply said female actors wanted for adult movie roles. No experience necessary, must be photogenic and eighteen years old, signed The Casting Shop, followed by an 800 number. Holly called the number and was told the time and day to go to room 135 at the Sleep Well Motel off I-275 at the Northgate exit. When she got there she was greeted by a male photographer and a woman in her forties who quickly reviewed the details of the "shoot," including signing some releases stating she was of age and that any photos or videos shot today were the property of The Casting Shop.

Always ready for an adventure and hopeful that her enthusiasm would get her a film role, Holly did whatever was asked. At first it was shots of her in various stages of undress. Then the woman said they needed to see how ready she was for the big time. She gave Holly a couple of sex toys and asked her to put them to use. Within minutes she was sexually involved with both the photographer and the woman. By the end of the night she had been videotaped performing a variety of sexual acts, alone or with partners. The whole shoot took less than forty minutes and she was told that they would be in touch. As she was leaving, another young woman was getting out of her car and looking for room 135. Needless to say, Holly wasn't contacted again.

Desperate for a job, Holly responded to an ad from Elite Personal Services. The office was in a small strip mall and she immediately thought she was in a doctor's office or maybe a lawyer's office. There was a receptionist sitting behind a sliding glass window. She was asked to take a seat and she saw several other attractive women coming and going during the half hour wait. When she finally met Mrs. K, the owner, she was surprised. Mrs. K looked like she could have been a mother on a TV sitcom, sort of like a Carol Brady type.

Mrs. K was very professional and when discussing the services that her employees provide. She never mentioned anything about sex and was clear that she expected all her escorts to be well dressed, clean, and personable. She would handle the financial arrangements and give Holly a small part of it. She said if Holly went above and beyond she could keep the tips. Holly knew there was more to the job when Mrs. K said that she would be scheduled for monthly medical check-ups with the company doctor.

By 9:00 p.m. Holly was standing with three other girls at the Delta House. The occasion was the Delts' Spring Chores – Time to Plant the Seeds. The frat house was pretty much as she remembered it. The overstuffed leather furniture in a large sitting room was almost dwarfed by a large walnut bar. The other rooms on the first room were equally large and consisted of a game room, dining room and full kitchen. The second and third floors were the sleeping and study areas. The bar was the activity hub, offering a couple of different kegs and a wide variety of spirits.

The four girls were not the only females there, but it was clear they were the scheduled entertainment. Besides beer, the boys were mixing up some wild cocktails they called "Seventh Heaven," which was a mixture of Benadryl, brandy, Quaaludes and Adderall. This drink along with some mid-level marijuana was quite a combination. Holly was never one to back away from a good time and willingly accepted all that was offered.

Within minutes, the girls were involved in all the "party" games. As planned, they all lost at beer pong and after drinking all of the cups proceeded to bet their clothing. The four girls were down to bras and G-strings when someone suggested Twister. Needless to say it was an excuse to grapple on the floor and in the process the bras and G-strings disappeared. Holly was getting quite stoned but still complied when it was suggested that she join the winners of the beer pong upstairs for more games. As she was led into one of the bedrooms, someone yelled, "Let's have a train!" The next hour was a blur with at least four of the brothers taking advantage of Holly in every way possible. The drug and alcohol stupor prevailed and Holly eventually drifted off into a hazy, coma-like state.

There were voices. She could hear them, but couldn't discern whether it was a dream. One guy was shouting to another, "Hold the door open so we can dump this skank on the lawn!"

Another voice was saying, "We just can't leave her like that—at least get her clothes and things."

She heard someone say, "Rob just help us get her outside the house. Hey, wait—where are you going?"

The Rob person answered, "I am going to call someone to come get her. We are not going to leave her in this state."

That was the last thing she remembered till she woke up in a different place. Forcing her eyes open, Holly recognized the furniture and knew she was in her living room, but didn't know how she got there. The wall clock showed 3:30 and since sunlight was shining through the window it had to be the afternoon. She thought, *I've got to think. I remember doing shots and taking some pills, but nothing else.* She had her dress on but was minus her bra and panties. She noticed her apartment key lying on top of her pocketbook, which was on the floor next to the sofa where she was lying. All she could think was, *Damn, I must have been really out of it, but I managed to get myself home.*

While lying on her sofa she could see the rhythmic flashing of her answering machine light. Hard as she tried the flashing light of the answering machine couldn't be ignored any longer. It was probably Mrs. K setting up another job. Pushing the answer button, it was definitely Mrs. K, but the message was not what she expected.

"Holly," said Mrs. K. "I bet you are wondering how you got home? Well, I did it with the help of a couple of others. I got called at 3:30 by some frat boy saying they couldn't wake you up and that I could pick you up on their front lawn. I called Shelby and she said that she and the other girls left about 1:30 a.m. and couldn't find you. So I had to leave my warm bed to drag your drunken, sorry ass back to your apartment. You are lucky I found your dress and pocketbook; otherwise I might have just left you on their lawn naked as the day you were born. I don't need this kind of grief. With all the college girls looking for extra money it is easy to replace you. I don't need to keep a drunken screw-up in my business, so I am done with you. The only place left for you is standing on a corner. Your last check can be picked up at the office on Friday and oh, your car is still at the frat house." The message ended without even a good-bye.

Holly tried to stand with difficulty and that was when she felt the dry crusty stuff on her stomach and in her hair. After thinking about it she realized it was sperm and thought "Oh shit, they went in bare back". She had some recollection of trying to push off guys that were over her but just a faint recollection. The hot shower cleared some of the cobwebs from her brain and the rubbing the warm washcloth over her body made her aware that she had been violated in more ways than she was aware of. As she opened the medicine cabinet to get toothpaste out, her eye was drawn to her birth control pills. Picking it up, she studied the case through blurry eyes. At first she thought she was counting wrong, but eventually realized that she had missed taking the pill for the last five days. She had forgotten her pill before and everything worked out. A couple of days shouldn't matter, right? What the hell would she do with a baby? She couldn't take care of herself, let alone a kid.

Meanwhile at the Delta Pi Theta house, Rob was recovering from the world's worst hangover. He spent the better part of the early morning hugging the porcelain. He was finally starting to feel like a human, but the previous day was a blur. He remembered starting the party early and never letting the mug attached to his wrist with a lanyard get empty. As he came to he realized his underwear was on backwards and he was sleeping on the floor.

The door to his room swung open and Blake, a fraternity brother, said, "Man, Rob, I have never seen you like you were last night. You were out of your mind. I couldn't believe how you banged that skanky whore that was here. You even went in bareback. Hell, you better see a doc to get some penicillin treatment going. Who knows what you picked up from her?"

Rob tried to focus. "What the hell are you saying? I don't remember anything from last night. Jesus, why weren't you guys looking out for me?You know I am only a few weeks from going to seminary and something like this could really mess up my life. Damn, do you know who the girl was?"

"Hell, we don't take names. She was hired from that escort service. She was so out of it that the girls she came with couldn't wake her, and then you went running all over the house trying to call the escort service. One of the other brothers finally called their boss. I guarantee you that she has no recollection of what happened last night. Keep your mouth shut and things will be okay."

Going to seminary was an important thing for Rob and his family. He had planned on being a preacher for years and knew he could preach God's word to those that hungered for it. People had always gravitated to him and often his relatives teased when they said he was a silver-tongued rascal. His mind quickly shifted to Michele. *Oh, my God , he thought, I am getting engaged in four months and could lose the woman I have loved for years. Thank God I am not seeing her for a month. That gives me a chance to get to the health clinic and make sure I am clean.*

Chapter One

The school bus drove slowly over the gravel road before finally stopping in front of the shabby, faded trailer that I called home. The bus driver had been making this run for the past eight years and she had trouble thinking that a girl like me, the one sitting behind her— who she thought was attractive, smart, quiet and well mannered, lived in such a rat's nest. In all there were 5 old style trailer homes placed somewhat in a semi-circle on a gravel parking lot just off the highway exit near the Flying K truck stop. At least one trailer was abandoned or seemed to be since the curtain had been blowing out a broken window and the driver hadn't seen anyone there for months. The others were not in much better shape. A couple of the trailers had skirting around the bottom but skirting was missing from most of them and you could see the old deteriorated tires under the trailer. Maybe 60 years ago someone thought they were creating a nice affordable housing site but that dream had long since disappeared and now it was just another hovel owned by a slum landlord.

As the driver opened the bus door, I gathered my books. I always chose the seat behind the driver because it was peaceful. All the other kids wanted to be far from the driver, so I really appreciated having an empty seat next to me for setting my book bag. This also allowed me better work space for studying during the fifty minutes in the bus each morning and afternoon. I was the last to be dropped off and the first to be picked up. Sometime I felt as if I spent half her day sitting in a school bus. I turned my head and looked at the driver as I stepped out of the bus and said the same thing as every other day: "Thanks Phyllis, see you tomorrow."

"Goodbye Delta, have a good night." The driver couldn't recall the girl ever saying much during the eight years she had driving this route. She never talked about home, trips or school activities. She seemed to be accepted by the other kids on the bus, but none of them were what you could call friends. The previous bus driver told her that Delta's mother was never around and he had heard she was nothing more than a prostitute working the truck stop. She couldn't verify that because in all the years she has dropped Delta off and picked her up she has never seen her mother. Typically, a school bus driver got to see all the kids' parents at some time but this wasn't the case with Delta, even when she was a seven-year-old.

The bus driver watched the tall, slender girl walk away from the bus. She'd never worn any make-up but it didn't matter because she had a natural beauty that make-up couldn't improve upon. Most girls her age were obsessed with their looks and always trying the latest hair color or lipstick, whereas Delta didn't seem to think about her physical appearance. The same thing could be said about her clothes. Delta's clothes were always clean, but they were worn and often the kids teased her about modeling the thrift shop clothing line. Delta would just chuckle and take it all in stride.

I climbed the rusted metal stairs to my trailer and dreaded opening the door. I never knew what to expect when I opened the door. Was my mother going to be there? Would she be high? Would she be angry? Would she be unconscious? I wasn't going to tell anyone about my mother any longer. There was a time when I told a teacher that my mother was drugged out when I got home and I ended up being placed in foster care. In fact, I was placed in foster care three different times over my fifteen years, but always ended up back home. Two of the foster homes weren't bad, even if I do say so myself. I really liked the Barretts, my second foster parents. I had fantasized living with the Barretts forever, but then at the next court hearing my mother came to the hearing cleaned up and I was sent home.

My last foster home still caused me nightmares. I was placed there when I was twelve. The parents treated me okay, but generally just ignored me. It was the biological son of the foster parents that caused the nightmares. He was sixteen when I was placed in the home, and large for his age. The first time he groped me I thought it was an accident and didn't think much of it. Soon he began saying sexually provocative things when he knew his parents weren't around. I had to be on constant alert walking by him because his hands would grab at my private parts. I may have only been twelve, but my body was really developed and on top of it I wasn't sexually naïve. I knew how my mother earned her money and had seen more than a few men stagger out of my mother's room. The paper-thin walls of the trailer didn't prevent me from hearing the groans, or the verbal commands given to my mother.

The first time my foster brother really touched me was when we were in the above-ground pool together. He cornered me along the edge of the pool so I couldn't get away. He then reached under water and roughly shoved his hand under the elastic leg band of my swimsuit. I screamed and hit his nose with my elbow, causing him to back away. He just laughed and said that he would get what he wanted and I would like it. I had learned a long time ago that the foster parents would never take my side, and so I never even considered telling them.

His threat came to pass within that week. I had been asleep for some time when I felt my bed shake. I quickly became aware that someone had pulled back the covers and was climbing into bed. Before I was fully awake, I felt a hand feeling my breasts and squeezing one of my nipples. I also felt as if my own body defied me, because the nipple became erect with his touch. It was at the point that I tried to scream only to be stopped by his huge hand over my mouth.

Keeping my mouth covered he said, "Shut up if you know what is good for you. You are mine!"

In the morning as soon as I heard the foster mother in the kitchen, I decided that I had to tell her what happened. The foster mother's reaction was immediate and severe but not the way I thought it would happen. The foster mother accused me of being a slut and tempting her son. She said, "I read the report and was afraid you would be a whore like your mother." She called her son into the kitchen and he told a complete lie about how I was always touching him. He said that last night I invited him into my room and tried to get him into my bed. Even when I showed the foster mother a blood stain on my sheet, she refused to listen to me.

By two o'clock that after noon my clothes were put a black plastic bag and carried to the trunk of the social worker's car. The social worker gave me the feeling that she believed me but added there was little she could do since it was my word against theirs and the county needed the foster beds they provided. I was taken to emergency foster care for the night. The next day with no other placement available I was delivered back to my mother's trailer. At that time, I vowed never to go into foster care again.

So now, at age fifteen, I reaffirmed my pledge of never going in to foster care another time. I didn't want to go through the hysterics all over again. I would do what it took to stay with my mother and I knew that meant taking care of her. I had cleaned up more vomit than most nurses saw in a lifetime. I made sure the few bills we had were paid on time. I scrounged enough money to buy food, which mainly consisted of TV dinners and packaged stuff that I could buy at the dollar store. I guess when all is said and done I had developed the philosophy that I would "play the hand that was dealt me."

I first heard that saying while watching the famous TV preacher turned politician Rev. Rob Strong. I accidentally turned the TV channel to his show one Sunday morning and started watching his show regularly. He talked about how we all had to make choices in life and we had to play the hand that was dealt us. How we played the hand made all the difference if we trusted in God. He spoke with such certainty and intent that I knew he was speaking to me. I started watching the show every Sunday. There was never a chance that my mother would bother me in the morning since my mother never got out of bed till early afternoon. Rev. Rob got a chance to speak to me every week and I listened.

Today I got an unexpected surprise when I entered my home because a big man was sitting at the kitchen table drinking coffee. My heart started racing seeing a stranger in the house. My past experience led me to believe that men were a threat and I had to be careful around them. I kept the front door open with my foot so I could run if there was any trouble. I timidly challenged him, "Who are you?"

"Whoa now, let's not get excited," he said. "I'm just a man that tried to help the woman that lives here."

"That woman is my mother—now what did you do to her? Where is my mom?"

He didn't say anything for what seemed like minutes, and just took a sip of coffee. He apparently had time to search through the cabinets and find the coffee and filter to go with the old coffee maker on the counter.

"She's in her bedroom, conked out I think. At least she was the last time I checked on her. I checked both bedrooms and one looked too much like a girl's. The other one had a bottle of vodka on the dresser and a carton of cigarettes next to the bed so I figured it was hers."

I fired back, "What do you mean, you put her there? She never lets anyone come home here. She promised me that she would stop bringing anyone home and that's been one of the few promises she has kept. If you think I don't know what she does over at that truck stop, you're sorely mistaken." In my mind all I could think was that she broke her promise again about bringing men home and I was so mad at her.

He didn't respond at first and then said in a quiet voice, "Well, I guess if you'll pipe down I'll tell you why I am here. I was walking back to my truck and saw her sprawled on the ground. When I couldn't rouse her, I started asking other truckers if they knew where she belonged. I have been driving this route for years and of course I knew who she was, every trucker knows the working girls. A couple of guys said that they thought she lived in one of the trailers over in the next lot. So I found a house key in her satchel, picked her up, and tried every door till I found one that the key opened."

As he talked I realized that the man probably wasn't a threat even though he was huge and had a bushy beard. My internal safety meter wasn't sending up the typical warning signals. He introduced himself as Oliver Kendall Jordan III, then he smiled and said, "But everyone calls me Ollie." For some reason I suddenly felt more at ease around him. Maybe it was the warm eyes that were attentive to everything I said, and I believed he was really listening to me and not talking much.

"Well, you can go now. I can handle things here."

"If you don't mind, what'd you say your name was?"

"Delta, my name is Delta."

"I just made this coffee and would like to finish my cup—then I'll be on my way."

I didn't think I would be able to move him out, so I poured myself a cup of coffee and sat at the table. It was a strange feeling for me. I had never been around many men except for my teachers and the one soccer coach I had when I was twelve. Oliver Kendall Jordan III—or Ollie, as he liked to be called—wasn't intimidating even though he looked like a bearded mountain man, but the situation of finding a strange man in my home most likely caused my initial fear. I had grown up never having someone to talk to, so trust wasn't easy for me, but before long I felt like I had known him for years. He seemed to be as comfortable with me as I was with him, and we both had little trouble disclosing personal information. I started telling him things about me that I never shared with anyone, not even my mother.

I told him about my dream of going to college and getting a degree in biochemical engineering. I talked about how I wanted to become a researcher and find ways to help people that are drug- addicted. Throughout my life I had watched my mother struggle to control her drug problems, and I'd seen how hard it has been for her on a daily basis. The reality is that she has never been able to win the battle. The times I was placed in foster care because of my mother's addiction always ended the same way. My mother would get clean—sometimes on her own, and sometimes through a treatment program. She knew what the courts were looking for and knew how to say the right things. My mother was always an attractive person, and sorry to say, sometimes good-looking women are treated differently by the courts. Each time they released me to my mother, she made promises that I knew she would never keep.

I talked with Ollie about the good foster homes I stayed in and how they made me feel as if I were really important. It was during those times and with their help that I actually began to believe that I was intelligent. They also taught social skills that made me the kind of kid teachers want to help. In fact, I realized at a young age that most teachers become teachers because they wanted to make a difference in a child's life. I learned how to become that child who makes a teacher feel like they are being successful. I said it wasn't dishonest, because I really needed their help, but at the same time I knew I was toying with the altruistic feelings of my teachers.

Even with no support from my mother, I blossomed in school. Academically, I was near the top of my class but around my classmates I still feel like a misfit. Tears came to my eyes when I told him that in grade school I was invited to only one birthday party, and that turned out to be a disaster. I arrived at the party without a gift and was picked up by my mother who was wearing a halter top, mini skirt, and go-go boots. That happened when I was in the fourth grade, and after that episode, the kids always whispered to each other and made jokes about my mother.

High school hadn't been much better. My academic success made me a favorite of the teachers but the other kids mostly ignored me. I didn't have money to go to the mall or even attend school events. The clubs I joined in school might look good on a college application, but they were the kind that other kids called Nerd Groups.

Ollie told me that he understood me really well because his life wasn't very different from mine except he got classified as a delinquent. He said, "I went through a bunch of foster homes and because I was always large for my age there was always some kid in the home or at school that wanted to see how tough I was. I finished high school while at juvie."

He then told me that he joined the Army and spent two tours in the Middle East during the Persian Gulf War and the Iraqi War. He shared that he came back a changed man and couldn't seem to fit in anywhere. Nothing seemed right, and he wandered through several jobs until he latched on to this job as a trucker. Being an over the road trucker gave him a combination of freedom and solitude so that he could manage each day. Ollie went on to say that he is an owner-operator, which means he owns the truck. He has no other address other than a post office box and lives in his truck 365 days a year except for the few times he visits his sister or on occasion stays in a motel.

"There are times when I think about settling down in one place, but all in all I am pretty content with the way things are. I must admit however that taking a shower at truck stops gets to be old," he said offhandedly.

Before I knew it, a couple of hours had passed. My stomach growled so loud that Ollie could hear it. It did remind me that it had been hours since I had eaten anything, and Ollie must have sensed it because he quickly said, "I'm starved—what about we order up a pizza?" I should have guessed that we would need more than a pizza, because when he placed the order he asked for two large Supremes, two salads, and an order of breadsticks.

After finishing off one of the pizzas I checked on my mother and found she was softly snoring and definitely seemed to be out for the night. Thinking everything was under control, I thanked Ollie for the pizza, but told him he really should leave. "Are you sure you're going to be okay?" he asked.

I replied, "I know what to do, and everything is under control. My mother has worked the truck stop since I was a child and there have been lots of times that she has come home in pretty bad shape."

As he left he said, "My rig is the bright green Volvo custom cab with Jordan Trucking on the door. I spend the night here at least one night a week so if you ever need anything, just to talk or help with something around the house don't hesitate to look me up. The trailers may all be different, but if you see a bright-green tractor, you'll know it is mine."

I climbed into bed after studying for an hour, and although I felt tired I also felt the most relaxed I had in a long time. I was woken once during the night when I heard cupboard doors slamming and a glass clinking against another. Lying there in the dark I heard my mother shuffle down the tiled hallway to her bedroom, but then I felt back into a sound sleep. The clock displayed 6:30 when the alarm woke me from a sound sleep.

Chapter 2

My morning routine was like a finely tuned machine. I'd been getting myself up and out the door for as long as I could remember. So my routine was pretty simple. First I made a pot of coffee and then headed to the bathroom to get ready for the day. I poured the coffee in my travel mug and if my mother had done any shopping, I made some toast. If there was an apple or orange I threw it in my backpack for lunch. I savored my morning coffee and usually could sip it on the bus and then slip the empty travel mug into my backpack before disembarking for school.

Maybe it was Ollie being in the house yesterday or my mother's drunken stupor, but today's routine was different. Usually I just left the coffee pot going for my mother, but today I gently pushed my mother's bedroom door open. Her room reeked of stale cigarette smoke and dirty laundry. I saw my mother stretched out across the bed with her head hanging slightly over the edge. I went over to the bedside prepared to adjust her position. When I reached out and touched her I was shocked to feel cold, clammy skin. I couldn't believe emotionally what I rationally knew had happened. My mother was dead. My first reaction was to grab and shake her, thinking that would bring her around, but her stiff body didn't respond.

I started to panic and before I knew it I was sitting on the floor hyperventilating. All the things that my mother had done wrong and all the times she failed me as a mother weren't important to me now. I was in a fog and couldn't find my way out of it. I don't know how long I was sitting there before I regained some semblance of calmness. Taking deep breaths, I felt the panic lift and my mind starting working much like solving a word problem in algebra.

To describe my reaction as flat and unemotional wouldn't be accurate, because I certainly reacted with emotion when I found her dead. The initial panic and tears that came with it were gone. Now I stared at my mother's body and my mind tried to wrap around the idea that I was truly all alone. If there was any sadness, it was because any hope of having a relationship with my mother was gone. I was indeed an orphan.

After several minutes I went into my default mode of behavior which was to intellectualize situations. I started to identify all the tasks in front of me. In my mind I created a check list of things to be done. 1. Call the police, 2. Find out about a burial, 3. List all the bills that are due, 4. Come up with money to pay the bills. Before I even got to five my list was falling apart again, but this time for a different reason. How could I call the police? They would immediately notify social services and I would be back in foster care. How would I even afford to bury her? Was there some agency that would pay for it? How could I pay for rent, lights, or food? The more I thought the greater the sense of dread filled me. One thing was certain—I couldn't just leave her where I found her.

As a turned my eyes back to my mother I noticed several empty vodka bottles along the side of the bed. The night stand had some prescription pill bottles lying on their sides. I didn't have a clue if the bottles were from a couple of days ago, and I certainly wasn't aware of my mother being on any prescription drugs.

I heard the school bus honk and knew that I wouldn't be on it today. I peeked out of the drapes in the living room and watched as Phyllis got out of her driver's seat. She climbed the rusted wrought- iron front step and knocked briskly on the door. I held my breath and didn't move. All the while I felt as if my knees weren't going to hold me, and they probably wouldn't have held me without the help of the wall. After a couple of minutes, the driver hurried back to the bus and was quickly underway. I felt bad making Phyllis take the extra time to walk to the house, but Phyllis knew that I never missed school and her action proved what I always thought—Phyllis looked out for me in ways that went above her job duties. When I walked past the kitchen table I saw the two coffee cups amidst the pizza boxes from last night. A plan started to develop.

Chapter Three

The gravel parking lot next to the truck stop still had several semi tractors and trailers there. I silently prayed that Ollie hadn't left yet. He had to be there if my plan had any chance of success. If only I could remember the name on the truck. Fortunately, I did remember that he said his tractor was bright green and there was only one green truck in the lot. As I neared the truck I breathed a sigh of relieve particularly when I saw Jordan Trucking on the door.

I couldn't see anyone in the cab, but thought he might be in the bunk. Stretching my long legs, I had no trouble reaching the step to the door. Putting a hand next to my face to block the glare from the early-morning sun, I looked in the window. I could make out some blankets on the lower bunk, but was disappointed Ollie wasn't there. *He must be getting breakfast*, I thought and jumped to the ground. Upon opening the truck stop door I saw several men and one woman sitting around a large U-shaped counter. There were also a number of people at the tables.

I quickly scanned the group and didn't spot my acquaintance from last night. However, I was aware that most of the customers had similar characteristics. There were lots of well-worn and soiled ball caps on their heads. The logos on the caps for chewing tobacco, racing cars, and American flags were mostly faded. There were a number of plaid shirts or tired-looking sweat shirts. Most of the men had full beards. I did find they all came in different sizes from really big like Ollie to so short and slender. I wondered how the short ones could reach the pedals. One thing they also had in common was their lack of need for social contact. Each person at the counter sat two or three spots away from their neighbor.

A quick tour of the aisles in the store proved to be unsuccessful. Every time I was at the truck stop I was intrigued by the broad selection of items available to the truckers. Briefly, I thought that a trucker could pick up a small selection of groceries, buy some sophisticated electronic devices for his truck, rent videos, or purchase underwear or any number of personal items. I also knew they could take showers and do their laundry for a price. The only place Ollie could be was in the shower room or lavatory. I stood next to the door leading to the drivers only section and asked the first person exiting if there was anyone else in there. The driver didn't go to any lengths to talk, but did quickly reply, "Nope."

As I walked back to the truck parking lot, I spotted the green truck pulling away. Running as fast as I could, I reached the side of the truck just as it was getting ready to pull onto the street. He obviously didn't hear or see me, because he pulled onto the street only to stop at the traffic light leading onto the entry ramp to the expressway. This gave me another chance. My side ached as I sprinted across the street toward the truck. Maybe it was fortuitous that I wasn't looking at the traffic exiting the expressway, because at that very moment I heard a screech of tires as a sedan slammed on its brakes. The irate driver laid on his horn, but it didn't bother me because I could see Ollie's face in the rear view mirror as he turned and looked back at me.

Ollie flipped on his flashers and climbed down from the truck. I was out of breath and panting heavily when I reached him. Choosing my words carefully I said, "Were you serious about helping me if I needed it?" At his urging he told me to climb in the driver's side because he didn't want Tiger, his dog, to get loose. As I opened the door I was thinking that a man like Ollie probably had a pretty vicious dog, maybe a pit bull. So I was ready for an attack and I was attacked by this white, fluffy, cute dog that couldn't weigh more than ten pounds.

Ollie shouted, "Move back, Tiger, and give her some room!" I slid across the driver's seat, all the while wondering if I was doing the right thing. Ollie said, "Before we talk, let me get off the road, and I'll need to drive down the road to find a good spot to turn around."

We ended up driving a half a mile before Ollie found a spot to turn around. For some reason I still wasn't feeling fearful around him and that surprised me. I had so little experience with men, and yet what I learned from my mother was that men will use you and then abuse you. Even feeling comfortable, the rest of my senses were still on high alert; because of the way my mother earned money many men thought I was part of the deal and that was always on my mind. I always appreciated the fact that unlike my foster parents, my mother never allowed a man to touch me. In his favor, Ollie didn't give off any sexual vibes. In fact, he seemed really more like a caregiver.

On the brief ride back in the truck stop, I learned that Tiger was Shih Tzu and permanently rode gunshot. Since I was in his seat Tiger had no qualms about sitting in my lap. Ollie explained that when you are on the road 24/7, a small dog works out best. He said, "Tiger gives me someone to talk to and the best part is that he never talks back to me."

After a moment I said, "I looked for you everywhere. At first I thought you were eating and then I stood outside the shower room. I was so scared that you were driving off. Thank you, thank you, and thank you for stopping when you saw me."

Ollie replied, "I was just walking Tiger before our next stretch. I'm supposed to pick up a load in Louisville this afternoon and deliver it to Atlanta. Hence, I'm on a tight time table, so why don't you tell me just what it is that has you all worked up?"

The reality hit me that I didn't know this man, and asking him to help me with this crisis was going to sound really crazy. The little confidence I had disappeared and I mumbled something that sounded like "Forget it, things are too messed up."

I reached for the passenger's door handle and was ready to open the door when Ollie's huge hand grabbed my arm. His grab wasn't done to intentionally hurt me, but his sheer size and rough hand caused me to cry out. "Just wait a minute now, and don't going running off," barked Ollie. "Something must have really got fucked up for you to come to me a stranger. Scuse my language—too much time talking to other truckers really screws up your polite conversation. However, if you need my help, you better start talking because I don't have all day."

I am sure he could tell I was rethinking my situation. There was no place for me to go for help. My neighbors, if anybody was renting one of the other trailers, were all transients. Even if they were more permanent, I didn't see them as the type of people that would do anything to help a neighbor. If I talked to a teacher, they would be required by law to report my situation. I had never been to church. The closest I had been to a preacher was my Sunday morning television time with Rev. Rob, and I knew he really wouldn't be able to help. The landlord couldn't care less about my situation as long as he got a check each month. This huge man with the large rough hands and bushy beard was the only possible solution I could think of.

The sigh coming from me was deep and endless. I turned sideways in the seat and stared at Ollie. Finally, I began speaking in a slow, hesitant manner, "You remember saying that if I needed anything all I had to do was look for the green tractor? Well, I really need something and I don't know if you can help." Ollie didn't say a word, almost as if he knew that anything he said would mess up what I was trying to tell him.

"I told you I know what my mother did to earn money. Did I tell you that lots of times she sold her body for drugs or booze? She usually had little left at the end of each week to pay the rent and utilities, let alone buy clothes or food. This morning when I woke up I made coffee as usual and checked on my mother before going to school." I really struggled getting the words out, as if my throat was being squeezed by a vise. "She wasn't breathing when I found her. Somehow she got more booze and there were a couple of empty pill bottles on the floor. I don't know what to do, and so I just left. I haven't called the police or anyone yet."

Ollie tried not to act as shocked as he must have felt. "Don't you have any relatives you can call, no aunts, uncles, or grandparents?"

When I shook my head no he said, "I can go back to your trailer and wait while the police come if that is what you want? I know how alone you must feel losing your mother."

A tear rolled down my cheek, the first time I had shed a tear since the barrage after finding my mother. "You don't understand," I said. "If I feel any loss it isn't really because my mother is dead. God, that sounds cruel to say, but the truth is she was never really there for me. I never knew when or if she was coming home. Some nights she would crash on the bed in a truck cab or go home with a Flying K customer. But I guess it just hit me that there will never be a chance for me to feel loved by my mother. It's the loss of something that I always dreamt and that is that she would get herself clean and we would form a relationship like Lorelei and Rory have on *Gilmore Girls*." Ollie didn't have a clue about that TV show I was referring to.

"I can't go back in the system, but I know they won't let me stay on my own. In another year I think I could apply to become an emancipated adult and that is what I am asking you. Would you be willing to tell the authorities you are my uncle and guardian? You won't have to stay here or really have any other responsibility. I know I could get a job at the truck stop—and before you say anything, not a job like my mother had. I could work the register or at the food counter. The job would give me enough to pay for my living expenses. I carry a 3.8 grade point average and I did that without any assistance from my mother. So I don't see maintaining a good school record as being a problem. What do you say? Are you willing to help me a little? You said you hated foster care, so you know where I am coming from."

Ollie sat quietly listening as the girl rambled on and thought *she was right about his hating foster care, but what she was asking was way beyond a simple request*. Ollie had always kept himself out of the public eye. He served his country honorably and avoided any trouble with the law. His life as a truck driver is really simple and there were no relationships to mess it up. If he needed female companionship, he paid for it. There were no other commitments once the money changed hands. Delta was asking him to make a commitment to her that was outside his comfort zone, and one he had no plan of doing.

"Look," Ollie said, "I think you are asking way too much of someone you hardly know—and besides that, I am like you and don't have nobody in my life. The difference between us is that I chose to not have anyone in my life. I recognize the fix you are in, but I can't help."

The tears rolled down Delta's cheeks and splashed on her top like it was raining. *Damn it,* he thought *the last thing I need is some girl crying—especially one hurting like Delta. I know what it was like to be alone but at least I made it through to the military. What would I have done if as a fifteen-year-old and how dangerous would it be for a young girl to work at the truck stop?* Most truckers were decent people, but they weren't the knights of the highway that so many people called them. Heck she could be taken advantage of so quickly it would make her head spin.

"Tell you what I will do," he said. "Just let me call my jobber and have him get someone else to make the haul today. Then I'll go back with you to your trailer and stay with you while the police and medical people are there. Okay?"

"Won't you lose your job and what about the money that comes with it." Questioned Delta.

Ollie was struck by the fact that this young girl in so much emotional pain would be concerned about a miserly little money. He answered, "Let me worry about my money. I have more than enough to keep me comfortable for a long time."

I had nothing to do but to concede the point that he would help me by calling the police and I would end up back in the system. Together we walked over to the trailer and started the arduous task of dealing with a dead body. Ollie said he had seen more than a few dead bodies while serving in the military, but nothing really prepares you for witnessing death up close. This was the woman he carried to the trailer just the day before and now she was no longer.

Ollie walked up to the closed bedroom door and pushed it open. He didn't know if it was the dead body stretched across the bed that made the room smell but whatever it was he didn't want to go any further. However, he thought *if the police were going to be coming to the house, I'd better get a closer look so I could answer questions*. There were empty vodka bottles and the prescription drug containers on the side table and floor. Using the edge of his shirt, he gingerly picked up one of the drug containers and saw that label had been torn off. There didn't seem to be a need to check the others because they would look the same. She either bought or swapped sex for the prescription drugs on the street.

Back in the living room, he told Delta that it was time to call 911 and then listened as Delta called saying, "I need help. I just checked on my mother and can't wake her up. I think she is dead. She isn't breathing. Please send someone." Obviously the operator was asking some identification questions as Delta responded, "Delta Anderson, My age? I'm fifteen. She's my mother, Holly Anderson. She's thirty-eight. 604 East Highway 6 in Greenville. It's the faded green trailer, second from the right. Yeah, it's next to the Flying K Truck Stop. Okay, I'll hold. Please hurry" She put her hand over the phone and mouthed that they wanted her to stay on the line until the first responders arrived. "Okay I will," she replied to the operator and then walked over to the door and opened it. Without thinking, Delta flipped the outside light switch even though she knew that light hadn't worked in years.

We sat starring at the floor while waiting for what seemed like hours, but in fact we heard the siren as it pulled up to the trailer after only ten minutes. The first one through the door was a Wood County sheriff's deputy. He immediately asked where the body was and followed me to the bedroom. He asked me to stay outside as he went into the room by himself and was there for several minutes then he came out he introduced himself. Both Ollie and I gave him our names, which he wrote down on a note pad. The trailer started to vibrate as a fire truck and EMT ambulance pulled up next to the sheriff's car. The roar of the vehicles and the red and blue lights cast a reflection on the kitchen wall and gave an eerie quality to the already dingy-looking trailer.

It may sound strange to say, but I actually had to talk myself out of being self-conscious about the condition of the trailer. I never had any friends over to the trailer because of how bad it looked, and it was rare that my mother ever had a visitor. I thought I had always done my best to keep it clean which was something my mother never concerned herself about. Today, at this moment, I was looking at things through a different set of lens. I saw my home through the eyes of the strangers entering the trailer for the first time, and knew that I could have tried harder. I noticed them looking a little too long at the stained sofa and the cigarette scarred table. One of them even tripped over a self-stick floor tile that was peeling up. Within minutes, there were five men in my mother's bedroom. My mind was going wild and I even stifled a nervous laugh as I thought how my mother would have loved to have five men in uniform in her bedroom at the same time.

The two fire fighters and two EMT left shortly after coming out of the room. I could hear parts of the conversation when they were in the bedroom and caught part of a phone call to what I assumed was a doctor. The deputy joined me shortly after that and started asking all the obvious questions. When did you last see her? Was she acting all right or complaining about feeling bad? Did she have any major illnesses? When there was a break in the questions, I asked why everyone had left. He responded, "In cases like this we need the County Medical Examiner to examine the scene and the deceased before the body—oh, I mean your mother—can be moved. After he gives his okay an ambulance will deliver her to the morgue."

With startling awareness, I realized how many questions I couldn't answer because I had no answer. "No, there are no other relatives that can be called. No, she didn't have a job. No, she doesn't have a family doctor. No she doesn't have a driver's license…at least I don't think so." The few I could answer other than name or age was about her substance abuse history. "Yes, she is a drug and alcohol abuser. Yes, she has been to rehab centers. Yes, she has tried to commit suicide before. Yes, she has a history of not coming home at night, and so on."

Ollie told the deputy all that he remembered. He found her lying on the ground in the parking lot. He found out she lived in this trailer and carried her home. He told him that I came home shortly after he carried her in the door. He opened the door with a key in the satchel that was on the ground by her. She was alive but really drunk when he carried her into the bedroom. Ollie also said that he just met me, and although he had seen Holly around the trucks, he had never personally met her. He told the deputy that I sought his help after finding my mother dead.

The deputy informed me that due to the fact I was a minor and because I didn't have any relatives that I could go to, he was required to call Children's Protective Services. I knew this would happen, but that didn't stop me from pleading with him. I tried to convince him that I was all right and could stay by myself. I explained the things I did on my own like getting up, going to school, washing my own clothes, going grocery shopping and cooking. I was getting more and more frustrated with his demeanor. The deputy wasn't going to change his mind and didn't seem to care what calling Children's Protective Services meant to me. He did tell me that he was remaining in the trailer till the medical examiner and someone from Protective Services arrived.

The medical examiner was at the trailer within two hours and spent less than a half an hour in the bedroom. While he was in the bedroom, an ambulance arrived and a man and woman pushed a wheeled gurney into the trailer. The two disappeared into the bedroom and in a short while wheeled out my mother's body in a black body bag. I overheard the medical examiner tell the officer that he didn't observe any evidence of foul play, but with the cause of death unknown he couldn't be more definitive until the autopsy. The medical examiner did stop on his way out to offer condolences and to say that he expected the autopsy to be completed by the end of the day tomorrow. If there were no complications the body would be ready for the funeral home after 5 p.m. tomorrow. I noticed that he addressed most of his remarks to Ollie only occasionally looking at me. I supposed it was a natural reaction to respond to the adult in the room, but he wasn't the responsible party.

Shortly after the medical examiner left, Ollie went out the door, saying that he would be back. I had no idea if he was coming back and really would be surprised if he did return. The silence in the room while the deputy and I waited for the CPS worker was deafening. After less than an hour I saw Ollie walking across the gravel from Flying K with a couple of bags. He lumbered up the stairs huffing and puffing like he had just run a mile.

Looking at me he said, "Sorry I was gone so long. I had to walk Tiger and wanted to make sure my delivery was covered. Since I was near the truck stop I picked up some lunch for all of us. You really should eat something, Delta—and I got enough for you too, Deputy." Ollie unpacked six hot dogs, an assortment of condiments, three bags of chips, and six assorted bottles of soft drinks. "I didn't know what you all like, so I got a variety—except for the hot dogs, of course." The deputy wasn't shy and took a couple of hot dogs, chips, and a soft drink out to the front steps. In between bites I overheard him on his phone telling someone—probably his supervisor—the current status of the situation.

Ollie also took a couple of dogs and sat at the kitchen table. After a minute I unwrapped the foil from a hot dog and took a small bite. "Thank you very much. You know you didn't have to do anything. In fact, I thought you were probably on the road again."

"I know I didn't have to do anything. Now eat more than that. Who knows when you'll get fed again."

Chapter 4

It was about 2:00 p.m. when the sound of a car pulling up to the trailer caused the three of us to turn our heads. Ollie stood up and went to the window where he could see a woman sitting in a tan four-door sedan that had a seal with Wood County Department of Social Services on the door. The social worker seemed to be going through some material in a folder on her lap. As she got out of the car, her appearance made his heart palpitate almost like it did in Iraq during a fire fight. In that moment he was brought back to his childhood and the experience he had being picked up by a social worker. Consciously he knew she was probably a good, hard-working woman, but emotionally she was there to take him away.

She sure didn't look like any social worker that he'd had as a child. This woman was tall, slender with long blonde hair, wearing a sweater, jeans and tennis shoes. She rapped on the door and then entered without waiting to be greeted. She immediately faced the deputy. "I'm Sue Sprague with the county. I believe we've met before. You sure look familiar. Maybe it was at one of the union meetings. Anyway I'm here to pick up hmm a Delta Anderson."

Before another word came out of her mouth, Ollie moved toward her with his hand out saying, "Good afternoon, I'm Oliver Kendall Jordan, III, Delta's uncle." The air was totally sucked out of the room for me. What did he say? I didn't know if she or the deputy were more surprised. Ollie turned toward me and winked an eye as if telling me to be quiet.

The deputy immediately responded, "Excuse me Mr. Jordan but the information I took from both you and Delta was that she had no relatives?"

"You must have written it down wrong. I'm her uncle. Maybe you misunderstood us because I didn't get along with my sister. I was a lot older than her and she was born about the time I was ready to leave for the Marines. Our parents died pretty soon after I left and we didn't see each other much. I'm a truck driver and only visited occasionally." I could see his mind going a mile a minute as he tried to remember things I had told him the night before while we sat around the table drinking coffee. "Yeah, Holly was a mess and I couldn't stand to see her drunk and on drugs. It killed me the two or was it three times that Delta was placed in foster care. I would have taken her myself—but you know, being on the truck and such."

The deputy looked totally frustrated and was obviously irritated with Ollie. "To tell you the truth I don't record things inaccurately. I wrote what you both told me. That being said, this is not my problem any longer. Miss Sprague, I am leaving now and I don't care how CPS resolves this mess. The police involvement is over as far as I am concerned." With that, he said goodbye and walked out the door. Ollie, Miss Sprague, and I were still staring at the door as we heard his patrol car kicking up gravel, leaving the trailer.

"Well, I need to get some answers from both of you. Let's go over how you are related again." The CPS worker's statement definitely put me at the crossroads of a major decision. It didn't look as if I could convince Ms. Sprague to let me stay in the house without an adult. So that meant I had two choices. One, I could admit that Ollie wasn't a relative and go back into foster care. Or two, I could go along with Ollie's lie and convince her that he was my uncle. I knew nothing about Oliver Kendall Jordan III. For all I knew he could be thief, druggie, or worse yet a child-abusing pedophile. Still, during the time I spent with him he had been nothing but a gentleman. He had gone out of his way and even lost work because of me. Besides, he'd probably just drive off and I'd be on my own anyway.

The next couple of hours were a blur. I followed Ollie's lead and agreed that my mother hated Ollie and didn't want anything to do with him. It soon became like a game I played in grade school where the teacher started a story and then each student added a sentence which could change the entire direction of the story. I even took the lead and told about the times "Uncle Ollie" stopped by to check on me when my mother wasn't around. I made up a story about how he showed up at my school to see me in Science Olympiad when I was in sixth grade. I said that school was a pretty safe place to visit since my mother never went to any events at school. Before it was over, our two stories had merged into what I thought was a pretty credible one.

"So Mr. Jordan, you are a truck driver that lives in his truck. How does that differ from Delta just being here all alone? You are away for days and weeks at a time."

"Well, Ms. Sprague, I agree with you. Delta can't be left alone. She needs adult supervision and support." My chin nearly hit the floor. He seemed to be building the case as to why he couldn't take care of me. Ollie's next words changed everything, including my life. "I haven't had a chance to talk to Delta yet about this, but I guess she's going to hear it the same time as I tell you." Looking at me, he said, "I told you that when I was out getting lunch I called my jobber. Well, what I was doing was checking to see if I could get a day route. I have an A+ rating with him and when I explained the circumstances he said he had the perfect solution. I can be based out of Greenville. I never wanted to do day routes before but now I have a good reason too. So each morning I go to the distribution center and deliver to Super Centers in Ohio, Indiana, Pennsylvania and Kentucky. Most days I'll be home between 6 and 7."

I didn't know if I could or wanted to trust my ears. This stranger was changing his whole life for me. I thought about what my mother always used to say, "When things are too good to be true, they usually are." She always thought there was no good in the world and used to call me a Pollyanna. God, my mother filled my head with crap.

What did this guy get out of this deal? However, I couldn't have been more surprised when Ms. Sprague said, "Okay let me run a records check on you Mr. Jordan and if it turns out all right then I'll have guardianship papers that will need to be signed. Until I get the records check cleared, Delta will need to stay in temporary foster care." The mention of foster care caused my heart to stop. I looked from Ms. Sprague to Ollie and back again, but to no avail.

All that was going through my mind was that Ollie would disappear or maybe he had a criminal record. I felt for certain that something was going to go wrong and decided to challenge the situation. I asked if I could talk to my "uncle" alone. Once given permission, I walked Ollie back to my bedroom. He was shocked by the difference in my room from the rest of the trailer. Whereas the other rooms looked shabby and worn, my room had a fresh coat of paint and was very neat. The bed had a colorful comforter on it. The dresser had some scars, but the cock-eyed drawers were all closed and the top had a couple of pictures and a clock radio on it. The desk was old and looked like something I picked up during trash day—which I had—and the numerous books and papers neatly stacked on the top hid the damaged top.

With the door closed, I faced Ollie and couldn't hold back my anger. "What the hell are you doing? You don't know me—how could you make those promises to her I know you are going to disappear as soon as she drives me away. I can't stand to be jerked around." My rant seemed to go on for hours even though it was only a few minutes. Ollie stood silently watching me and let me blow off steam.

"Are you through?"

"I am, unless you have something to say."

Ollie proceeded to talk in a quiet voice so that Ms. Sprague couldn't hear. "You are right. I had no plan on staying, but when I saw that woman walking toward the trailer I could only think about what happened to me in foster care. I told the truth when I said I checked with my jobber and made arrangements for someone to cover my delivery, but I thought it would be for a couple of days. Now that I have made a commitment, things have changed. I want you to know that I keep all my commitments. So as soon as she says the word, I will be your guardian, and will be home most nights. I don't have the slightest idea how to be a father and Lord knows I didn't learn anything from my own father. I can tell you this about me. I don't carry much anger, I am honest and treat people fairly, but I don't take any crap from anyone either and that means you. If this is going to work, you have to commit to it too. I thought this is what you wanted me to do?"

"Where are you going to stay?"

"Delta, I am sure that Ms. Sprague will be checking on your living situation regularly. I plan on staying here. So you tell me which bedroom you want and I'll take the other. I will be here most nights but it will be probably closer to 7:00 p.m. than 6:00 p.m. I will give you my itinerary so you will know where I am traveling too each day. If for some reason I can't make it back here I will call. You are going to do the same with me. I will need to know where you are at night, like with your boyfriend or if you are staying overnight somewhere."

"Ollie, first off, I never stay anywhere other than home. I am always here studying. Second, I don't have a boyfriend. In fact, I have never been asked on a date—not that I am interested in going out with anyone. Third, I want to keep my same bedroom. There are too many bad memories with my mom's bedroom. I know I would have nightmares thinking about her body lying in the bed. But if you are going to be staying in the house, I want a lock put on my door. You seem okay to me, but most men do at first. I don't know if I can trust you—at least not right now."

When they returned to the living room, Ms. Sprague was completing a phone call. "I found an emergency foster home placement for you, Delta. They can keep you for a few days—now before you get excited, I think my checking on Mr. Jordan's record won't take that long, but you never know. So I would like you to go pack a bag with clothes for five days. Don't forget your toiletries, and school books. Oh, you can bring your laptop or iPad."

I stood silent and then walked toward the kitchen. When asked where I was going, I told her, "I have to get a trash bag to pack my stuff and oh, I don't have a laptop, iPad, or even a cell phone." After pulling a black trash bag out of the drawer I walked to my bedroom, still wondering if this was the right thing to do.

Ollie and Ms. Sprague stood in silence for several minutes. They could hear Delta in her bedroom opening and closing drawers. They also watched her as she came back into the kitchen and got a smaller zip lock bag. She waved it toward Ms. Sprague and said it was for her toiletries. Ollie shook his head and said, "She doesn't even have a suitcase for her belongings? My god, talk about feeling like you're trash."

Ms. Sprague answered him in a very quiet voice. "I'm afraid it's not unusual at all for kids in foster care to carry their belongings in trash bags. Every once and a while some organization or church goes on a shopping spree and buys suitcases for all the kids in foster care, but for some reason they disappear. Once the kids arrive at the foster home or at juvie, their clothes are unpacked and the bags put in storage. Most kids move pretty frequently and a lot of their things never make to the next placement."

Ms. Sprague turned to face Ollie and looked directly into his eyes. "These foster kids have it rough and I can tell Delta has a lot going for her. If what she says about her school attendance and grades is true, she is the exception. I have been doing this work for several years and I can't explain how she could come from this troubled home and have made it, but it looks like she did. But to be certain, I am going to check with school authorities."

Getting very serious, she firmly addressed Ollie, "If you think for a minute I believe you're her uncle, you are kidding yourself." Ollie started to talk and she cut him off. "I care about the children I work with and I don't think Delta's best interest will be served by foster placement at this point in her life. So I am going to play along and do a comprehensive records check on you before making you her legal guardian. If I find anything out of line in your record, Delta will go to permanent foster care. If your record comes up clean, I will let her stay in her house, but rest assured I will be checking this house all times of the night and day. I am doing this because I think it is the right think for Delta, but it is my ass that is on the line. So you better fulfill your commitment."

I came back into the room just as Sprague was finishing lecturing Ollie and I could see his face had turned red. "What was she saying to you?"

Ollie replied, "She was doing her job and making sure I was serious about my commitment. Just so you hear my answer, too—I want both of you to know that I always keep a promise. My commitment to you is like money in the bank." Then looking at Ms. Sprague he said, "And as far as my record goes, you aren't going to find anything."

Chapter 5

Ollie watched the two of them walk to the county car and felt a hollow pit in his stomach as the worker put Delta's trash bag in the trunk. He had been driving alone for years and used to be proud that he kept himself free from personal relationships. In the military he enjoyed the camaraderie, but never formed close personal bonds. He received the reunion notices from his former troop, but never responded. What was different this time? How could he change his life for someone he met just a day ago? He was thinking, *this is crazy*, but at the same time he never thought about going back on his decision. In fact, he felt really good about this decision.

Ollie walked over to his truck and drove it to the front of the trailer. "Well, Tiger, you are going to learn what it is like to sleep in a house. Now let's go inside and see what needs to be done." This time as he entered the trailer he saw it with different set of eyes. Now it was the eyes of someone who would be spending the next couple of years living there—or at least until Delta was emancipated. The place was barely inhabitable, and in reality his sleeping cab was looking better all the time. "Well, Tiger, the longest journey begins with the first step, so here we go."

Since he knew he would be sleeping in Holly's bedroom, Ollie attacked that room first. The sheets and blankets were pulled from the bed. He had seen a washer and dryer in an open closet space by the bathroom. The bi-fold doors that once enclosed the laundry closet had been removed or fallen off, allowing a clear view of the really old appliances. Evidently they hadn't been run in a long time, because the water hoses had both rotted out. Since the sheets weren't going to be cleaned, he started hunting for an extra set that he could use tonight. After looking in every closet and on every shelf, he concluded that there were no extra sheets. His search did reveal that Holly and Delta were living in the worst kind of poverty or as his mother use to say "dirt poor." Everything was worn or tattered and all he could think was that any money Holly got from selling her body went for drugs.

Using a trash bag from the kitchen, he preceded to clean up the bedroom. The floor was covered with everything from liquor bottles to magazines. The two jalousie windows were covered by old blankets that were nailed completely tight around the window frame and didn't allow any outside light or ventilation. Once the blankets were down he was able to open a window, allowing a breeze to enter the space. The smell of dirty laundry and stale cigarette smoke dissipated slightly.

By the time he had cleaned up the room, fed the dog, and gotten something to eat for himself, it was nearly ten. Grabbing a blanket and removing only his boots, Ollie stretched out on the bed. He must have been physically or emotionally exhausted because he was asleep within minutes. The sun shining through uncovered windows reflected off the dresser mirror and acted like a spotlight in his eyes. As he awoke and tried to get out of bed every muscle in his body screamed in pain. The mattress must have been as old as the washer and dryer.

It took several minutes before he could stand and move freely. Of course he also knew that handling a big rig all these years had done a number on his knees, back, and shoulders.

Ollie hadn't been totally honest with the worker and Delta. His jobber had said he thought he could get Ollie on day trips only, but it wasn't a sure thing. It was only after Ollie called a couple of times the next morning and intimated that he would find another jobber that he had the firm agreement. His stomach was in knots the whole morning…and it wasn't just about the trucking job.

He knew that his record was clean. He received an honorable discharge and never even had a traffic stop. If they check with his jobber they would find he was loyal, consistent, and a hard worker. Nevertheless, the longer he waited for Ms. Sprague to call, the more he thought she had found something. What if she was able to open his juvenile record? He certainly wasn't an angel as a kid.

Ollie thought about his father, a World War II vet, who came back from Europe angry and depressed. Hell, he wasn't a father. The only time he came near him was to slap him around. His mother was a lot younger than his father and was more like a little bird and would never think of talking back or challenging his father. He could tell she didn't like the way his father treated him, but she seemed powerless to do anything about it. Ollie never feared his father and was always standing up to him even if it meant getting hit in return. One day when his father came at him Ollie was two inches taller and thirty pounds heavier. Ollie's mother had to pull him off his father, and that was the last time his father messed with him

The next morning after spending one night on Holly's old mattress, he knew it wouldn't work for him. There were several things that needed to change in the house and after making an extensive list he headed out to do some shopping. His first stop was at a furniture store that promised same-day delivery of a full bedroom set including a new king-sized mattress set and frame, and they would pick up the old one too. Leaving the store, he saw a nice student's desk on sale and asked the salesperson to add that to the delivery. Next, he visited a Supercenter where he bought a number of new blankets, linens, and towels, along with several other household items. His next stop was to an appliance store where he bought a new stackable washer and dryer. They could deliver in two days and would pick up the old appliances free of charge. The final stop was to his cell phone company where he bought a new phone for Delta and added her to his account as friends and family. By the time he was back to the trailer he had spent nearly $4,000. *Oh, what the hell*, he thought. *What else am I going to do with the money?*

The new mattress set and desk, as promised, arrived by the end of the day and Ollie had the bed made with his new sheets. Waiting for the delivery had given him plenty of time to box up Holly's room. Not knowing what Delta wanted to do with her mother's things, he visited the convenience store and got enough boxes to do the job. After filling them, he stacked the boxes in the living room. Then he waited. Still no phone call, and once it was 5:00 he knew the office was closed for the night.

After walking Tiger, he thought he'd watch some TV. He had a small 10" TV in the truck but only used it with his DVD for watching movies. Once in a great while he spent some time in the truckers' lounge to watch a sporting event such as auto racing or football. He also never watched network TV, but kept up on what was current through talk shows on Sirius radio. To his way of thinking Sirius Radio was one of the best things for truckers since air conditioning. He could listen to the same station all day and never lose the signal or pick up any number of interesting shows. Sometimes he listened to music, but most often liked talk radio.

The TV was in the living room and was still a boxy style. *So much for a flat screen with stereo and HD*, he thought. The worst part was when he tried to get a station, he only got snow. Noticing the antenna wire was not connected he thought the problem was solved. With the antenna he managed to get four stations but a couple had ghosts and none were clear. After attempting to correct the problem Ollie gave up and decided to try out that new mattress.

The mattress was huge, particularly because he was use to a single bed size in the cab. It handled his 6'5" 320-pound frame really well. He had to lift Tiger onto the bed. Tiger always slept with him and he knew there would be complaints from the dog if he changed things now. As he lay on his back, his head was spinning about everything he had to do the next day, but sleep came eventually.

Ollie woke up totally rested. The new mattress was really worth the money and getting a king size was the frosting on the cake. For the first time ever he actually fit in the bed. The 500-count sateen sheets added to the sensual feeling. Ollie thought that he had just gotten lazy living in the truck. Most nights he just covered himself over with a blanket.

After finishing two cups of coffee he figured he was ready for the day. The first thing he did was place a call to the phone number on Ms. Sprague's card. It immediately went to voice mail where he left a message. "Ms. Sprague, this here is Ollie Jordan, Delta's uncle and I was hoping you would have some information as to when Delta can come home? I know you must be really busy but if you can call me, I'd appreciate it." With the call out of the way, Ollie started another to-do list.

This list consisted mainly of projects that needed to be done around the trailer. He could handle all the projects on the list but he would have to run to Home Depot to get some basic tools and supplies. He also thought about the lousy TV reception and figured he could solve that problem with a visit to the cable company. Since he had his cell phone on him, he figured he could go out in the morning and still be available by phone if Ms. Sprague called him. Before leaving, he measured one sheet of glass broken in a window. He also did another walk through to make sure he didn't miss anything, until he stepped on the rusted and broken front steps. Eyeing a better set of steps at one of the abandoned trailers, he added Rustoleum and a paint brush to the list

He had never been shopping in Home Depot for tools and supplies and was blown away by the items for sale. Before he knew it his cart was over flowing. A couple of hammers, an open-ended wrench set, three pairs of different size pliers, a rechargeable drill, a utility saw, electric tape, and the list went on.

His next stop was the cable company, and that was when the amount of choices overwhelmed him. The salesperson asked how many channels did he want and which channels? Did he want HD? What about internet? Did he want a Wi-Fi router? Did he want a bundle with TV, internet, and phone? The choices seemed endless. The whole time the salesperson was talking, Ollie was watching the flat screen TVs attached to the wall. He ended up taking out a contract for the basic extended channels, which the salesperson said would most likely have all the popular channels for his niece and him. He also added the internet with a Wi-Fi router.

The salesperson gave him the name and location of the most affordable and best computer and TV store. Ollie was surprised how easy it was to spend money, and it still didn't bother him. He bought a 54" flat screen with HD, the wall bracket to hold it, and a nice laptop that the salesperson said was ideal for a high school student. With his truck fully loaded he headed home. He had to chuckle at himself for calling that dump home.

After unloading the truck, he started on the first project, which was dragging the old steps to the abandoned trailer and dragging the better set back to their place. He steel-brushed the stairs and then painted them with black Rustoleum paint. He actually felt rather proud of himself as he stepped back and looked at the job.

The rest of the day flew by as he worked on one project after another. He even was able to replace the glass, which surprised him. Probably challenging him the most was attaching the TV bracket to the wall. He had all kinds of trouble finding studs and then assumed that a trailer this old probably only had 2x2 studs. By late afternoon he collapsed on the sofa and Tiger gleefully ran around the room in celebration. The cable company said they would be there between 10 and 2 the next day, so he was ready. Actually, he couldn't wait to use the new TV so he went to the truck and got his DVD player along with a couple of movies. He selected *Talladega Nights* as the movie to watch, not just because Will Ferrell always cracked him up. He liked John C. Reilly and could see himself sitting at a bar and tossing back a couple with that boy.

He had drifted off when the ring tone on his cell phone woke him. He saw that it was Wood County calling, and when he answered he heard Ms. Sprague's voice. She told Ollie that Delta would be home tomorrow, but it probably wouldn't be till after dinner because she had other appointments first. She also shared that the coroner had released the body and Delta agreed to release it to a medical school. This eliminated the cost of a burial and also fulfilled Delta's wish to advance medical research. When Ollie said that he was be more than glad to go get her Ms. Sprague cut him off and said, "I told you I would bring her to you and that is how it is going to be." The timbre of her voice let him know in no uncertain terms he shouldn't challenge it.

After hanging up he looked at Tiger and said, "Well, boy—I guess you are going to see what it is like to live in a home for at least one more night."

Chapter 6

There wasn't much said during my ride to temporary foster care. Ms. Sprague seemed to be lost in her own thoughts, much the same as I was. We did talk about my mother's body and I was pleased that she could be used for medical research. It was one thing less I had to think about. For me the greatest concern was still about getting a handle on the most recent turn of events. I guess the big unknown for me was whether Ollie was for real. Regardless, I had to look out for myself and to do what I needed to earn some money. If I could save up money over the next several months, I could go for emancipation when I turned sixteen.

To break the silence, I asked Ms. Sprague if there was a chance I could become an emancipated adult. Her answer surprised me. She said, "Delta, Ohio doesn't have an emancipation law. No one is able to file a legal action to have a minor emancipated or legally on their own under the age of eighteen. There are two temporary ways in which a minor can be out of the custody of their parent. Either join any branch of the Armed Forces or get married. Do you want to do either of those?" I must have looked dumbfounded, as she added, "Didn't think so."

It took over a half an hour to reach a large farm house on the edge of Wood County. I could tell the farm hadn't been worked in years. The equipment sat rusting in the fields and around the barn. The fields were overgrown too. The worker explained to me that this was the only family that had an opening, and if all went well I would be out of there in a few days at the most. It wasn't that the farmhouse and barn were dilapidated, because they obviously had been cared for at one time. They just looked like someone walked away, allowing everything to fend for itself with the elements.

I waited with my bag of belongings while Ms. Sprague rang the doorbell. An older lady opened the door and greeted us as if she were expecting us. The interior of the house was neat, but looked like something out of a museum or one of those historic houses people tour. I remember going with my school class one Christmas to see a bunch of historic houses in downtown Greenville. This house had a similar feeling.

The older lady introduced herself as Mrs. Switalski and asked me to sit in the entry way while she talked with the worker. They went into another room and I could tell by listening to bits and pieces of the conversation that things weren't going smoothly. Eventually they both returned and Ms. Sprague said, "Mrs. Switalski was surprised you were a teenager and so large. She generally doesn't foster older children, except for Bonnie who has been with her for six years." I could tell the foster mother felt stressed, but soon she seemed ready to go on and told me to follow her.

Ms. Sprague talked as we walked and explained that the Switalski's ran a short-term emergency placement group home. I would be the sixth child in placement. Four of the kids were under ten, except for Bonnie, and she was fourteen. She said I would be staying in a room with Bonnie. There was nobody in the room when we got there. Mrs. Switalski pointed to the bed I would be using and said I could put my belongings in the bottom drawer of the dresser. She then said, "Well, let's go find the other kids—and by the way, most kids call me Ma; it's just easier than saying Switalski." Her foster mother mode must have kicked in because she seemed like a kind, caring person, which wasn't the way I felt when we first met.

She led us to the kitchen which could aptly be described as a large farm kitchen. There was something cooking on the stove and a big old table had already been set. Looking out the window, I could see some young kids running around the yard chasing after chickens. In one corner of the kitchen sat an old man in a wheelchair. Ma spoke to him slowly and clearly, "Dad, this here is Delta. She is going to be staying with us a few days." He made a sound, but I couldn't tell if he understood her or not.

Then she said to me, "Mr. Switalski had a major stroke a few years back. He understands things, but can't talk much, so don't fret if you think he is ignoring you." She showed me around the rest of the house. To accommodate the wheelchair, it was apparent they had turned one of the downstairs rooms into a bedroom. The last room we entered was obviously the place when everyone spent most of the time in the house. There was a TV, plenty of chairs for sitting, and two work desks against the wall. Sitting in an overstuffed chair was a girl that had to be Bonnie. She was sitting with her arms crossed in front of her and eyes staring at the floor.

Ma stood in front of her and said, "Bonnie, I want to introduce you to Delta. Remember I said a new girl was coming for a few days and she would be in your room." Bonnie jumped out of her chair. Although she was younger than me, she must be two inches taller and maybe fifty pounds heavier.

Bonnie yelled, "You lied. You said it was a little girl that I got to be like her big sister. You lied, lied, lied!" and with than she ran from the room.

The foster mother looked at the worker and said as she chased after the girl, "See, I knew this would bother Bonnie. This is just what I didn't want to happen."

I was wondering what my next couple of days were going to be like. The supper meal went fine. I met the four other children. They were all boys and seemed easy to get along with. Bonnie didn't let her feelings for me interfere with her meal, because she loaded up her plate. Ma had made some kind of noodle and hamburger dish that was really tasty. Mr. Switalski was wheeled up to the table by one of the boys and Ma put a bib around his neck. She then proceeded to feed him while barely getting anything for herself. She looked very tired and unhappy, but she treated all the kids well. Again, I could tell she was trying to be a caring foster mother.

After dinner, everybody had a chore to do. I was assigned wiping dishes. The boys were clearing the table, putting away dishes, feeding the dogs which I hadn't met yet, and a couple of other chores that had something to do with the chickens. Bonnie sat at the table glowering at me and not saying a word. Ma must have sensed that I was wondering why Bonnie didn't have chores when she said, "Bonnie takes the trash out." It seemed like a pretty simple chore for a big fourteen-year-old, but maybe that's all she could do.

The first two days were uneventful although Bonnie seemed to be glaring at me most of the time. The bus picked me up at the end of their road and my day in school was easy. The routine in the foster home was easy to follow and after supper I settled down to study. Finally, after an hour I got into bed. Bonnie stared at me all evening and it was difficult getting to sleep knowing she was watching me from about five feet away. Shortly after drifting off to sleep, I heard a yell, but before I was fully awake something slammed into the side of my head.

When I regained consciousness, the lights were really bright, white light almost. The strange part was I could only see the light with one eye. Something was covering my other eye, but I couldn't move my hands to remove the cover. I couldn't figure out where in my room the light was coming from. Was my mother shining a light at me? It was difficult thinking because the side of my head was throbbing.

A woman wearing a nurse's uniform moved next to me and took hold of my wrist. She talked in soft comforting tones and told me I was all right. I was in a hospital recovery room following emergency surgery. She asked my name and address, what school I attended and who was my favorite teacher. She then asked me who the President of the Unites States was. I must have answered the questions to her satisfaction because she said to someone else, "She is coherent and responsive."

I asked her what happened and why I was in the hospital. "You don't remember anything?" she replied. I told her the last thing I remember was falling asleep and then feeling this terrible pain in my head. The more I talked, the more I remembered, so I added that I woke up because someone screamed. I also knew that I was hit in the head by something.

I could hear lots of voices, but they seemed to be in other parts of the room. Painfully I turned my head and could see there was a white curtain separating me from other people most likely recovering from surgery. While the nurse was still standing next to me jotting notes down on a clipboard I asked her why I had surgery. She answered, "I'll let someone else explain what led up to the surgery; that isn't my responsibility. What I can tell you is that you were in surgery today to repair a cracked eye socket, which is why your left eye is bandaged. Surgery was successful—I'm sure your mother will be relieved." With that she turned and said, "Your worker is outside talking with the doctor now. They will be in to tell you about the surgery and answer any questions."

Sure enough, a doctor and Ms. Sprague stepped into the room. While he quietly read the chart at the bottom of the bed, Ms. Sprague walked up to the side of the bed and patted my leg saying, "You're going to be okay, Delta."

When I tried to talk, the doctor held one finger up, giving the universal gesture of "just one second." Once he finished reading he came close to me and said, "Delta, I'm Dr. Gates, ophthalmologic surgeon, and I was called in because of the kind of injury you suffered. I had to repair what is called the orbital rim. This bone was fractured by a direct impact to the face. Usually I see this kind of injury commonly caused by an automobile dashboard or steering wheel during a car crash. In your case it was a baseball bat. Because a great deal of force is required to cause a fracture of the orbital rim, I had to check for any other extensive injuries to other facial bones. While you were unconscious, a neurologist evaluated your EEG because sometimes we see injuries to the brain. I specialize in the surgery you needed. Because of the damage limited to the eye area, I had to be sure there was no additional injuries to the eye itself, such as the optic nerve which is responsible for vision, along with the eye muscles, the nerves that provide sensation in the forehead and cheek, and finally the sinuses around the eye and the tear duct."

"The good news for you is that your eye and the optic nerve were not damaged. I had to do surgery to repair the fracture and to make sure your face stays beautiful. Before you ask any questions, I want you to know that there will be a recovery period. You will have extensive bruising, there may be blurriness in your left eye, but I expect that to improve on its own in a few days. The stitches will have to be removed in about a week and I would like to do that at my office so I can do a complete vision examination. Now do you have any questions?"

Did I have questions? I had plenty of them. So I started, "I don't know how I got injured and you say it was a bat. The last thing I remember was going to sleep. How could I get hit with a bat?"

"I'm afraid that is a question your worker will have to

answer, sorry. Do you have any medical questions?"

In answer to my many questions he told me I was on a saline drip to ensure I didn't become dehydrated following surgery. I would have some pain and discomfort but it should respond nicely to Tylenol 3. I could also ask to see him if the pain was too severe. I would need to wear an eye patch for a couple of days to rest the eye. Since the surgery wasn't invasive, I could be released late that afternoon, depending on how things looked. He used very fine stitches and most of them were at the bottom of the eyebrow, so there shouldn't be a noticeable scar. The nurse would remove the bandage over the eye before I was discharged. He was out the door as soon as he answered my last question.

Ms. Sprague obviously came to the hospital straight from bed. She had no make-up on, and was wearing sweats and a stocking cap covering her hair that looked so beautiful earlier in the day. She seemed really nervous and was almost stuttering as she tried to explain what happened. On Call Staff at the county received a call from Mrs. Switalski, saying I had been injured and EMT had been called. She called Mrs. Switalski, who informed her that the ambulance had just left for the hospital and I was were unconscious because of a head injury.

"At first she tried to tell me that you fell out of bed and injured your head, but quickly dropped that story. She told me that Bonnie had hit you with a bat while you were asleep. Bonnie then panicked and ran to Mrs. Switalski room. Mrs. Switalski had to stay at the house because of the other children, but she seemed more concerned whether Bonnie would be in trouble."

It was clear to me that Ms. Sprague was nervous because she pushed the placement even when Mrs. Switalski said she didn't want a teenage girl. She knew Bonnie would get intensely jealous and that's what happened.

I was seething and didn't hold back. "This is just what I was telling you. I could have been all right at home—but no, you had to put me in foster care. Now look at me. Why did you have to do that? Why couldn't you have left me alone I would have been okay?"

After a few minutes either I was out of steam or the effect of the surgery was taking a toll on me, because I was exhausted and my head was killing me. It was about that time that another nurse came in to check me and said that in a few minutes I would be moved to a regular room. She gave me a pill and I didn't remember any more as I drifted off to sleep.

Opening my eyes, I could tell I was in a separate room, but didn't remember getting there. I did remember my talk with the doctor and Ms. Sprague. And more important, I remembered how I got there in the first place. I could see a tray next to my bed with a covered plate and a drink with a straw. I reached for the drink and found the first sip was like a balm for my parched mouth. My love affair with water was interrupted when a nurse said, "Well, glad to see you joined us. I was beginning to think you were going to sleep the whole day through."

She told me it was a little after 1:00 and that the doctor

would be in to see me after 4:00. If all was well, I would be released and could go home. I thought, *Go to whose home?* I definitely didn't want to return to the Switalski home and would resist it with everything in me. *I guess I'll have to wait and see what is planned for me.*

Chapter 6

Ollie was in a sound sleep when his cell phone started ringing. He was still a little disoriented, sleeping in a strange bed in a house, and wondering why his jobber would call him after they agreed he would be off a week. The only calls he ever received were from his jobber. When he looked at the caller I.D. the name Sprague appeared. Checking the time on his phone he saw it was 5:20 a.m.

"Hello?"

"Mr. Jordan?"

"Yes."

"This is Sue Sprague from Child Protective Services. Sorry for calling you at this hour, but I am at the hospital where Delta just got out of surgery and wanted you to know about it."

Ollie exploded with a barrage of questions, and it was only after he stopped to take a breath that he realized how worked up he was over the incident. His first response was to go there right away, but then he thought, *I don't mean anything to Delta, so she wouldn't be expecting me*. Sprague must have read his mind because she said, "Delta is sleeping and there isn't any need for you to get here this early. I think what will work best is for you to meet me 4:00 at the hospital. Just ask for Delta's room number. I'll have the temporary guardianship papers for you to sign and you can take her home from the hospital."

After he agreed to the plan, Ollie lay back in bed thinking he would go back to sleep, but instead his mind was racing a mile a minute. He couldn't focus on any one thing and went from outright anger at Delta being hurt in foster care to fear about taking care of another person. Taking a few deep breaths, he knew sleep wasn't going to happen, and he got up to make some coffee and walk Tiger.

The rest of the morning was spent continuing with the list of chores and waiting for the delivery of the washer and dryer. The cable company was also going to be there between 10 and 2. While waiting he dragged the old washer and dryer out the front door. As he looked at the two old pieces on the ground, he chuckled thinking it looked like the stereotypical picture you see of West Virginia. Here he was, living in a dilapidated trailer with old appliances gracing the front yard.

Grabbing the vacuum, mop bucket, and hot soapy water he attacked the tile floor in the house. The floor under the washer and dryer was filthy, but once he washed it I could see what the tile must have looked like when it was new. Once he finished Delta's floor, he put on the new sheets he purchased and stood back to appraise his work. Shortly before noon everything was done. The washer and dryer were delivered and installed. The cable guy finished his job and ran through how to operate the cable box and the Wi-Fi. The cable guy even helped Ollie with the Wi-Fi connection on the laptop and the cell phones. Things were looking up.

After a quick lunch and hot shower, Ollie was ready to go to the hospital. As he was climbing into his truck it occurred to him that Delta's injury might make it difficult to reach the steps of the truck. Thinking it through, Ollie took out his cell phone and called information for a taxi. It took the taxi over a half an hour to get to the trailer, which meant it was after 4:00 before he reached the hospital.

Just from stepping into the hospital foyer, his stomach turned over. He had never spent much time in the hospital, but all of it was bad memories. However, the real reason he had butterflies in his stomach was the idea of seeing Delta. She had been injured and had surgery. What could he possibly say to her to make her feel better? He didn't even know her. Would she think he was a fool even coming to the hospital? He was never good in any social situation, and this situation was way out of his comfort zone.

He passed a gift shop on the way to the reception desk and stopped to look at some of the items. There were magazines, candies, and flowers, but he didn't have a clue as to Delta's interest. Then he saw a plush yellow stuffed animal. It was a rabbit and for some reason he thought it would appeal to a teenager. So standing at the reception desk with a yellow rabbit under his arm, he asked for directions to Delta Anderson's room.

When he reached her room, Delta was sitting on the edge of the bed. For a good-sized teenager, she looked small and weak. The strong, self-assured teenager he saw two days ago was gone and in her place was a rather helpless child. Ollie saw her face reflect surprise that he was here and maybe even a fear of him. He handed Delta the rabbit and mumbled something about being sorry she was hurt.

Delta thought, *I didn't know what I was thinking or feeling when Ollie stood at the door. Here is this huge man holding a yellow stuffed rabbit and looking nervous as all get out. I don't know who was the most nervous, him or me. I didn't really know this man and now I had to depend on him more than I ever wanted to*. He mumbled something about her being hurt and she mumbled back that she didn't really remember what happened. With that, she looked at Ms. Sprague, hoping that she would take the lead. It was then that Ollie seemed to notice her for the first time.

She stood and asked Ollie if they could talk in the hall. Delta could hear her voice talking quickly as if she wanted to get this part over with. They seemed to be going back in forth, but she couldn't understand much and Ollie raised his voice and said, "How the hell could you leave that poor girl there? You should have brought her back to the trailer. She would have been safer there." Ms. Sprague must have worked it through with him because Ollie quieted down and in a short while they both came into the room.

She spread out some papers and starting explaining what they were to Ollie. Basically they were assigning temporary guardianship to Ollie as Delta's uncle, which also meant he wouldn't be compensated like a regular foster parent. Ollie read them and asked a few basic questions, which surprised Delta. He must have been thinking about his responsibilities. He asked what he would need to get medical information and would he have the right to sign for medical treatment.

She responded by saying, "Yes, but Delta does also qualify

for Medicaid."

He also asked about school and whether he needed any special documents to communicate with the school. Delta thought, *Wow, the man has really taken this seriously.* Before signing Ms. Sprague asked if he was sure this is what he wanted to do.

Ollie said, "I am very sure. I know that I will be her guardian till her eighteenth birthday and I don't want her in foster care ever again."

A nurse went over the discharge papers and explained how to care for the surgical wound. She changed the bandage and dressed the wound so Ollie could see what had to be done. This had to be kept dry and the bandage could be changed once a day. She also had a prescription for Tylenol 3 to help with any discomfort and a patch to cover the eye. It didn't look like rocket science and between the two of them he thought he had it handled. He didn't like it when she suggested that he would need to get additional health insurance, but at least he would think about it.

Ms. Sprague explained that she had handled the bill and it would be paid by the county since Delta was a ward of the county at the time she was admitted. An attendant showed up at the door with a wheelchair and Delta was told that she would be pushed to the discharge area. They waited outside under the portico while Ms. Sprague retrieved Delta's things from her car. She was expecting Ollie to go get his truck, but when she looked for the green truck she couldn't find it.

Shortly after Ms. Sprague returned, a cab pulled up next to them and Ollie said, "Our ride has arrived." He told her that the truck's step up would have been too hard to reach after the surgery, and hence the cab.

During the 25-minute ride back to the trailer, Delta was at first quiet, as was he. It was a very uncomfortable emotion because she was feeling guilty for trapping this man. She decided an easy ice breaker was to ask what Ms. Sprague said about the injury.

"What did she tell you?' he replied.

"She said Bonnie, the foster child, hit me with something while I was asleep and it hit my head."

He became really animated and said, "Bullshit, that girl took a baseball bat and clobbered you over the head. I was so angry when she told me I was ready to do battle. Although she wasn't very clear about the situation she did intimate that the foster mother was opposed to having a teenage girl because of the way the other girl acts. I was ready to have you sue for damages when she bartered a deal."

Delta got mad and spit back, "What did she have that she could make you keep silent about my injury? It had to be something good."

Ollie, with his eyes staring at the cab's floor, said, "She told me she had done the search on me and there was no way I was a blood relative of yours. However, she still wanted me to be your guardian only if I let the incident in foster care drop. Her rational was that the other four kids in foster care would be hurt if the license was revoked and the Switalski Group Home was better than the average home."

What he said stung. In order for Delta to stay in the trailer she had to allow Ollie to become her legal guardian. Ms. Sprague wouldn't approve his guardianship if Ollie raised a stink about the injury. The whole thing seemed crazy, and Delta was sure that another reason to bury this incident was because she forced Delta's placement in the home against the foster parent's wishes.

The green truck blocked her view of the front of the trailer, and it wasn't until she got out of the cab that she saw the stairs had been painted. On closer examination, they weren't only painted—they were a totally different set. She then noticed her old steps haphazardly placed at the door of a vacant trailer. The light by the door was on for the first time in years. Stepping inside the house looked, smelled, and felt different. It wasn't that it was just clean, because it also seemed brighter. Delta realized that some of the light was coming from her mother's bedroom. Ollie must have taken down the blankets covering the windows.

Several minutes were spent discovering all the changes. Delta immediately noticed the boxes stacked in the living room. Ollie, seeing her gaze, told her those were all her mother's things. He wanted to make sure she had a chance to go through them and keep the things she wanted. She nodded her understanding. Then she noticed the large flat screen attached to the wall.

He said, "Living in the truck, I never had a chance to watch

TV on a big screen, except in the driver's room at truck stops. I thought we both could enjoy it? It's all hooked up to cable so you can get 166 channels, although there have only been a handful that I will watch. The rest seem like crap."

Delta told him she never watched much TV. Little did she know that she would prove that statement a lie over the next few days of recovery. As she walked down the hallway, she noticed the bi-fold doors were back on the laundry closet. Ollie pulled them open to display a new washer and dryer. He said, "Energy efficient. I thought we both could use these instead of going to a laundromat."

Her eyes strayed into her mother's old bedroom and saw a huge king-sized bed with a beautiful comforter on it and all new furniture. The windows had new blinds and were even clean. She could smell the fresh air coming through one of the open windows. "Wow, you have been busy," she said.

The final surprise was her bedroom. Her old rickety desk was gone, and in its place was a new- looking maple desk with a center drawer and three drawers on the right side. On top of the desk was a new desk lamp which sat behind a laptop and a cell phone. Delta's heart was racing like she had run five miles. She didn't know what to say and immediately thought about what he would want from her in exchange for the new items.

Ollie spoke first. "Before you say anything, let me get my two cents' worth in. The TV and the washer-dryer are for both of us. They'll make my life easier too. The desk was too good of a deal to pass up. I saw it when I was buying my new mattress. The laptop and cell phone are for you. No strings attached.

The cell phone is essential for us to keep in contact particularly with that Sprague woman doing drop in inspections. The laptop is to make it easier for you to compete in school. When you turn eighteen, I want you prepared to meet the world."

Ollie then told her about the wireless router and briefly showed how she could access the internet through the laptop or the phone. He said they were on the friends and family plan, so she had plenty of minutes, and calls between them wouldn't count on the usage.

On her bed, she saw a stack of new towels, washcloths, sheets, and blankets. "I hope you don't mind, but I threw out your old stuff. It was too ratty to even give to Goodwill. You have a couple of sets of sheets and three towel sets, so that should take care of you. Someday when we have time I'll take you to the Linen Store and you can buy a new comforter and curtains. Ollie opened up the lap top and did a search for comforters. "Look here," he said, "there are four stores within ten miles of us. Aren't computers a wonder?"

Who was this man? Fixing up the trailer, buying new things and even caring about new linens all surprised Delta. Now he used the computer like he a pro. She had to ask, "How did you learn to operate a computer?"

"Well, honey, being a truck driver doesn't mean you don't keep up on things. I have had unlimited data on my cell phone for years—and didn't you notice the computer screen facing me in the truck? All my transactions with the trucking companies are done online, and even my log is on the computer. Gone are the days of a handwritten journal and two sets of logs."

The next few days seemed to drag by slowly. Delta realized the impact of surgery and for a couple of days she slept half the time, and when she wasn't sleeping, she was lying on the couch watching TV. Tiger had grown really fond of her and spent a lot of time curled up under her arm on the couch. Maybe he sensed she was injured, because the attention he gave her was over the top. Delta only hoped that Ollie didn't get jealous.

The three days also gave Ollie and Delta a chance to start a relationship. His changing the dressing on her head was a challenge for both of them. Allowing a stranger to care for you in that manner is a form of intimacy neither of them was used to. They set down some ground rules. Ollie would buy the food, but Delta would have to cook it. Since she would be cooking, he expected her to make a grocery list. When she tried to tell him she couldn't cook, he said, "Learn, you have a brain, the food channel and the internet." So she did watch the food channel and found she enjoyed it.

Ollie was old-fashioned in lots of ways. He said they both would be fully dressed in the house at all times. No walking around in underwear or skimpy things. They each were responsible for their own laundry. They would keep each other informed of their schedule on a daily basis and if for any reason one of them was not home by 7 p.m. it was that person's duty to call the other. He said she had to be in by 9:00 on school days and 11:00 on weekends. He also said that she couldn't date till she was sixteen, and then only after he met the guy. Some of his demands were silly, like no dating, since nobody had ever asked her out. Sometimes he made her angry, like the single-handed way he decided she would be the cook. Overall, though, she was cool with his suggestions.

Delta was glad to be back to school, not that anyone noticed her. There were only three people who were aware that her mother died, and they were the school secretary, her guidance counselor, and the principal. A couple of kids asked about her head. She no longer had the bandage or eye patch on, so it was hard to miss the ugly scar and stitches. Ollie drove her to school the first day so he could introduce himself to the school administrators. For a guy that never had been a parent, he sure did more for Delta than her mother ever had. She had to admit that at lunch she loved looking at the other kids' eyes grow wide when she took out the most recent edition of the Apple iPhone. Maybe having Ollie as her guardian was going to be all right.

Chapter 7

I rolled over and hit the snooze alarm on my clock radio. I had been using the new sheets for seven months and I still loved the luxurious way they felt when I stretched my toes as far as I could and felt the sleek satin-like material surrounding my foot. It seemed like Ollie had been living with me forever. Here I was in the fall of my sophomore year and everything was going really well. Not that there hadn't been rough patches. Ollie wasn't the neatest guy around and I got tired of cleaning toothpaste off the sink every day after he used it. He also could be moody. There were times when he would say only a few words the whole evening.

Then again, there were the moments when he was kind and thoughtful. One day he gave me a Pandora bracelet and after that once or twice a month he gave me a charm to add to it. He must have really struggled to think of charms to give me, since I didn't have a whole lot of activities to build on.... The first charm was a dog representing Tiger. Then he gave me a semi and trailer. The most recent were nondescript charms like a flower and a star. The half-dozen charms I had on the bracelet were starting to look nice, and I appreciated his thoughtfulness.

Probably the worst moment happened right before school got out in the spring. David, a boy from my chemistry class, asked if I would tutor him. We would stay after in the library and study. Often, he would wait with me for the late bus and that was when he talked about other things. The late bus was a special one for those kids in after-school activities. Sometimes he asked lots of questions about my living arrangement, and I could never tell if he was being nosy or just trying to find out more about me. I knew he was aware of my mother's death, because he had made a comment about it in earlier conversations.

After a couple of sessions, he said that he would drive me home, which I appreciated. The first day he drove me home he reached over and gave me a kiss on the lips. It was sweet and gentle and my first real kiss from a boy. Things changed the next time he drove me home. The kiss became more passionate. His tongue was in my mouth before I knew it. I was actually enjoying the kissing and when his hand went up the inside of my top I didn't stop him. He was pretty nimble with his fingers and with one hand he unhooked my bra. His hand felt smooth on my breast and I started to get really heated up as he twisted my nipples.

The sweet and gentle side stopped and he grabbed my hand and put it on his crotch. I could feel his hardness, and the outside of his pants was hot and damp. I pulled my hand away and he went the other way, shoving a hand down the front of my jeans. When I fought him off, he became angry and starting talked about my mother the whore. He said I should at least let him get to third base. I started yelling at him and trying to get out of the car when all of a sudden the driver's door was yanked open. A huge hand came in the car and pulled David out of the car by his belt. Ollie had David up against the car and I could see the kid was scared shitless.

I tried to talk to Ollie and he only looked at me and said, "You get your ass in the house now." I ran to the house while trying to keep my bra from falling down and holding my jeans together because they had come unbuttoned. I didn't know who I was madder at—Ollie or David. I thought I could have handled David, but I wasn't sure. In another way, Ollie had come to my rescue, and there was never a doubt about what Ollie thought was right or wrong. I also realized that for the first time in my life I experienced what a normal parent's reaction was when their child was in over their head. Regardless, it took a good week before we were back to interacting normally.

All things considered, it had been a good seven months. My grades had never been higher and for the first time I didn't feel like the pitied poor girl. Today was my sixteenth birthday, and even though I wasn't expecting anything, I was excited. Ollie told me he would be home early and we could go to Red Lobster for my birthday dinner.

I just loved Red Lobster, particularly the rolls. Ollie arrived home at 6:00 and we were at the restaurant by 6:30. After dinner we were driving home when he passed the exit for our trailer. When I told him he missed the exit he said, "I didn't miss it. I've got a little surprise for you." In about five minutes he pulled the truck into a driveway and left his lights shining on a cute little ranch house. There was a porch across the whole front, an attached garage, and beautiful landscaping. Ollie jumped down from the truck and told me to follow him.

From his pocket he pulled a set of keys and opened the

front door. "What are you doing?" I asked.

"Relax, Delta, this is our house. I bought it as a surprise for your sixteenth birthday. Let's take a look. I've wanted to get away from that trailer for a long time, and a realtor helped me find this ranch-style house that I think is perfect for us."

I was thunderstruck by Ollie's statement that he bought a house, and followed him inside still in sort of a daze. The house was beautiful, and my eyes were tearing up as I stood in the living room. Ollie continued talking and I could tell he was excited because he rarely rambles when he speaks. He said that he liked the house because it was only ten years old and was in great shape. There were three bedrooms. Two bedrooms were on one side and a master bedroom and bath on the other side. The kitchen had all new appliances and was open to the living room and dining area. There's a laundry room off the kitchen that led to the garage.

He opened sliding doors off the dining area that led to a deck and fenced in back yard perfect for Tiger. I couldn't think of anything that wasn't perfect about the house. In a spontaneous gesture, I ran to Ollie and threw my arms around him. In my seven months of knowing Ollie, that was the first time I had hugged him. At first he stood like a big lug, but then softened his stance and put his arms around me.

Ollie said, "I was thinking that I would take the master suite and you could have the other two bedrooms and full bath. One of the bedrooms could be your study room or media room and the other your bedroom. I don't care how you use them. There is a full basement, but it is unfinished so it will be for storage or maybe a workshop. I always wanted to do some woodworking."

"Ollie, the only thing I am not sure of is the school bus run. Did they tell you when and if the bus comes out this far?"

Ollie had a huge grin on his face and said, "You know, I didn't even ask them about that, because I have another gift just for you."

I followed him into the laundry room and watched him open the garage door. There was a bright-red SUV in the middle of the garage. Ollie put in hands in his pocket and pulled out a set of keys. If the house wasn't enough to blow me off my foundation, this car was. I started bawling like a baby and for the second time in a matter of minutes I hugged the giant of a man and kissed his cheek. Although he was trying to hide it, I saw a tear run down his cheek. This seemed to be as big of an event for him as it was for me.

"There's only one thing, Ollie. I don't know how to drive and don't have a license."

"Don't worry about that, honey. I have this weekend off and that will give us a chance for driving lessons in between moving."

I was walking on air the next couple of days and could hardly wait till the weekend. Friday after school Ollie told me to pack up my stuff and to think about what I wanted to have moved because Two Men and a Truck were coming first thing in the morning. I started telling Ollie what stuff I planned to move when he interrupted me and said, "You really don't want all that shit, do you?" It ended up the only piece of furniture we moved from my room was the new desk. The movers had a pretty light load carrying only my desk, assorted boxes of miscellaneous and kitchen items, Ollie's bed and mattress set, the washer and dryer, and the flat screen TV.

Ollie and I drove over to the house to open it for the movers. While we were waiting, he made a list of all the little things we would need. You know, the kind of things you never think about when you are moving into a new place, like additional towel racks, doormats, and the like. After the movers dropped of the few items he said, "Come on, let's go shopping and try out that car."

Ollie gave me a set of keys and it scared me. Did he think I was going to drive right now? He cleared that up when he told me it was my set of keys for the house and car and that he would keep a set of keys. I got into the passenger side and Ollie climbed behind the wheel. I didn't even know what brand of car I owned until that moment. Ollie told me that I had a Jeep Cherokee and it was two years old. He explained that he wanted a car big enough so that I would be safe. The car had 4-wheel drive so it would be good in the snow, but only 4 cylinders so it wasn't too powerful. He then showed me the proof of insurance and registration in the glove box. The final thing he did was hand me the insurance policy and title. I knew it was for real when I saw typed next to "owner" Delta Anderson. This started Ollie's style of driving instruction, which lasted for several days. Every time he got behind the wheel he told me what he was doing and why he was doing it.

We spent the day shopping for furniture and other items. By midafternoon we had bought furniture for every room. The only thing that Ollie demanded was that the furniture be strong enough and large enough to handle his size. By late afternoon I was ready for my first driving lessons. Ollie wasn't the easiest teacher, but he sure knew how to teach for safety. That night was the first time I slept in my own house, and I don't think I ever slept as good, even sleeping on the floor.

By the time I went to bed on Sunday I had driven for several hours and Ollie thought I would be ready to go for my driver's license in a week. I stayed home from school on Monday to accept the furniture delivery. Once the new furniture was in the room I rearranged it a few times before I found something the felt right. The TV was located in a perfect place so that I was able to watch it from the kitchen. Dr. Phil and then Ellen kept me company while I roasted a chicken, made mashed potatoes, and cooked up some green beans. By the time Ollie got home at 7:00 p.m. all the furniture was in place and it looked and smelled like a real home. I was Little Miss Homemaker.

Ollie took me out driving every night the next week for an hour or two and in no time I was ready for my driving test. The written test was simple and mostly logic, but the road test was scary. To be in a car with a stranger that was watching my every move and jotting notes down on a clipboard made my heart beat so fast I thought he could hear it. I must have handled my anxiety all right, because when we finished he handed me the paperwork so I could get a temporary license. The next day, more than a few kids' heads turned when I pulled into the student parking lot at school. In high school every kid knows who is driving what car. So I am sure my cherry-red Jeep was talked about a lot that day.

TWO YEARS LATER

I was out of bed in a flash and eager to get to school. Today happened to be Virtual College Visitation Day and I was excited. This Virtual College Visitation was something new the universities were using to recruit more students to their campuses. Over twenty colleges and universities were participating in a day-long activity for seniors. The idea was to provide as many seniors as possible information about their school. The virtual tour helped in your selection process. As an honor student, I had some options other kids didn't have in that a number of the universities did a separate presentation about their Honors Colleges just for academically talented students.

Ollie had already left for the day, but there was a note on the fridge reminding me that he was taking me out for a birthday dinner. Ever since my first birthday together, Ollie tried to do something really special. Last year he took me to New York City, where we did all the things tourists do like visit the Statue of Liberty and the National 9/11 museum and memorial. We also went to a Broadway musical and saw *Wicked*. Ollie suffered through the musical, but he did it for me. Still I couldn't imagine how he would beat the last two birthdays.

I was engrossed with the universities' video presentations, but the decision for further education wasn't difficult for me. For some reason, ever since I was a young child I wanted to go to the University of Michigan. I never talked much about it to classmates, because most of them bled scarlet and gray for

OSU. I was particularly interested in biochemical engineering and the U of M program was one of the best in the world.

That evening I drove the two of us to Red Lobster, which had become our favorite place to celebrate birthdays, holidays and other good things. Ollie was never much of a talker, but tonight he seemed more quiet than usual. While we were waiting to be served he gave me two wrapped packages. When I opened them I saw a beautiful set of diamond earrings and an open heart necklace. I felt like a little child that was disappointed when Santa didn't bring the gift they really wanted. The jewelry was beautiful and I embarrassed myself by having these crazy thoughts that I wanted something more exciting.

While we were having coffee, Ollie started to say something a couple of times and stopped. He looked really nervous and ill at ease, which was not typical for the big man. Most times he was really sure of himself. With gentle encouragement he started talking and when he did I knew why he was nervous. Ollie was talking about the elephant in the room that both of us pretended wasn't there. I listened, but was afraid of what he was going to say.

"Delta," he started, "you are now eighteen and you know what that means? You are free to go on your own. I no longer will be your guardian."

I didn't know what to say. Did he want me out of his life? For the past three years I had never felt so safe, and was this all going to change? I interrupted him to say, "Ollie, I know what happens now and if you want me to go or if you want to take off I understand. You have done so much for me I could never repay you. So I understand if you want your life back."

There was sweat running down his face and he was struggling to find the right words. Finally, he reached in his pocket and handed me a set of papers. "You and I have got along okay, haven't we? Both of us have no family and I have found during these last almost three years that I don't want to go without family anymore. You don't have to answer me right now, but I want to know if you would like to be adopted by me, because I would like to adopt you."

Well, he did it again. I was totally blown away by his suggestion. I really thought he wanted to get out of the relationship and wasn't expecting this. He wouldn't let me answer him and said that I was to sleep on it. I thought that he might have been fearful of what I would say.

I unfolded the papers and saw that he had already filled them out. There was a copy of the law that spoke to many of the issues. Adoption meant I could inherit his estate and remain on his health insurance while I was in college. It was set up for people like us that had a guardianship or foster care relationship. There was no home study needed and basically it was signing the papers and giving them to the court for their approval.

Ollie went on to add, "Delta, even if you choose not to be adopted, this house will always be yours. Both our names are on the title. I did that back when I purchased it, so just in case something happened to me you would always have a home. And, although our relationship started a little funny, we have moved beyond that. I can honestly say I love you and want to be your father."

Tears were running down both our cheeks by the time he finished talking. I got up from my chair and threw my arms around him while kissing his cheek. "Thank you Ollie, this is the nicest birthday ever." As we were driving home I thought that this was more like a marriage proposal in that we are both adults and each has a say in whether either wants a legally binding relationship.

In bed I thought about Ollie's offer and realized that over the last several months I had started to think that Ollie would always be part of my life. I had unintentionally accepted him as my family and thought of course he would be there. Ollie took his guardianship seriously. He never missed a teacher parent conference. He attended my choir concerts even though I was sure he was bored silly. After the incident in the car with David, Ollie even tried to have "the talk" with me. Even when he went shopping, he may have been uneasy if feminine hygiene products were on the list, but he picked them up for me anyway. The more I thought about it, I realized Ollie had become my father a long time ago.

Ollie was sitting at the kitchen table the next morning. I went over to him and knelt down beside him saying, "Ollie, I have thought a lot about your offer last night and if you are willing to have me, I would love to be your daughter." I was swept up in his arms and swung around the kitchen like a rag doll. I guess that signified that he still wanted to go through with the adoption.

I signed the adoption papers and we talked about the last

name. I didn't see any sense in changing my last name. It would be confusing to my school mates and may cause problems with the college applications I have completed. Ollie didn't have a problem with my decision. He said, "I always assumed you'd take your husband's name when you married anyway."

I looked at him and laughed as I said, "I guess you don't know me as well as you thought, Dad!"

The next few months flew by as I was busy at school. As a member of the National Honor Society I was active in a volunteer project to paint a non-profit food bank. I also decided to take a job— and it wasn't about the money, because Ollie always made sure I had money. The truth is I wanted to experience what it is like to work for someone. I chose Starbucks because I liked their company philosophy. I would also be able to transfer to a Starbucks when I went to college and there might be some scholarship help available.

One of my favorite school experiences was the parent breakfast for all graduating seniors. Ollie was like a kid getting ready for the breakfast. He even bought a new sport coat and shirt to wear that day. Each graduate had a chance to introduce their parent or parents and I thought the buttons on Ollie's shirt were going to bust when I stood up and said, "I would like to introduce my father, Mr. Oliver Kendall Jordan III."

I had been accepted to every college I applied to, but nothing thrilled me more than the day I received the thick envelope from Michigan. Other students told me if the envelope is thin, you didn't get in. It had always been a dream and now it was coming true. Between scholarships I had earned, some grants from Michigan, and help from Ollie, I didn't see any financial roadblocks to college.

I can't say I was sad to leave high school. Most of my experiences in school were pretty terrible. With the move from the trailer to our own home and the stability that Ollie gave me at home, things improved. I don't know if the kids sensed it and treated me differently, or if I felt better about myself and could finally make friends. I had three or four girlfriends that I spent time with and I even dated a few different guys. I never went all the way with any boy that I dated, although we did do some heavy petting and got to third base a couple of times. Sex had been forced on me once and I had made up my mind that I wasn't going to give it away till I was ready.

Ollie visited Michigan's campus with me and went to the parents' program for incoming freshmen. He was excited about me going to college but also a little sad. Ollie said, "Now that you are going away and won't be home at night, I think Tiger and I will go back on the road again." I knew that he didn't want to be in the house by himself and also knew that he made a lot more money when he was driving long distances, but our relationship was solid, and with FaceTime on our phones, we would be communicating a lot.

Chapter 8

FOUR YEARS LATER:

I can't believe I am in my senior year of college. Engineering school at Michigan has been a challenge but I think I figured it out. My grades have been very good and I realize that to pursue my dreams I have to go on for a doctoral degree. The combination of a degree in chemical engineering and a medical degree will put me in position to join a major university as a researcher. I am ready for four additional years of study, particularly if it will get me where I want to go.

My birthday is tomorrow and Ollie has already made plans to take me out to Red Lobster. I don't know how I would have made it through the last four years without Ollie. Just knowing he had my back allowed me the freedom to reach for the stars. I knew if for some reason things didn't pan out, Ollie would be there for me. We saw each other only about once a month, but on that occasion it always felt like we had never been apart. He would tell me where he had been traveling and I would tell him about my classes and other details about school.

One of the most difficult times for me was when Ollie told me that Tiger died. I had grown really fond of that little mutt during the few years we lived together and it was like losing a good friend. Ollie bought a little Chihuahua he called Ruby, but it wasn't the same for me. Ruby was clearly Ollie's dog, and every time we were together—even when I was home for vacations—Ruby did nothing but bark at me.

Ollie had kept up the house and I used it fairly frequently. It was only a couple of hours from Ann Arbor and I liked being able to get away from the campus every so often. Most times I was there by myself, but once in a while Ollie managed to have the same weekend off and those were the best times. There is something about knowing you have a home to go back to that really takes the pressure off. Even in my worst times at school I had this fantasy that I could always go back home to Greenville and things would be okay.

During my sophomore and junior years I had a steady boyfriend. Todd was in the mechanical engineering program and really driven to succeed. Maybe our relationship was doomed from the beginning because we were too much alike. He was driven to achieve and had a difficult time relaxing. The one time I met his parents I was very uncomfortable, and I felt they were evaluating me the whole time we were together. I could tell by their pointed questions that they disagreed with my upbringing by making statement such as living with a truck driver must be a challenge or it was terrible that your mother died without a guardian plan in place.

On a few occasions I took him to my home for the weekend, but that didn't make much of a difference. He and Ollie got along all right as long as they were talking about cars. The rest of the time neither of them attempted to communicate. It sounds shameful to say, but the best part of our relationship happened in bed. Intimacy was always a big question mark for me. Could I become intimate with a man? Before Todd I wasn't sure if I could ever have a normal sex life after my early experiences, but he was a confident and gentle lover. I felt relieved that my mother's behavior and my previous sexual assaults hadn't damaged that aspect of my being.

I don't know if Todd and I broke up or just drifted apart. He graduated a year ahead of me and took a job with PCA in Dallas. The promise we made was that we would do FaceTime every other day and get together every other month. We only got together one time and the FaceTime idea didn't make it past two weeks. I guess he wasn't my true love, because I didn't feel bad about losing him. However, I will always be thankful to him for showing me that I could have a wonderful, loving relationship with a man.

Ollie met me at my apartment that I shared with three other girls. They all knew my father and really seemed to like him. He in turn got a kick about out the attention he received from college girls. None of my roommates knew that Ollie only became my legal father my senior year in high school. They knew my mother was deceased and just assumed he was my biological father. I never cared to correct them about their misconception, because in truth Ollie was my only father.

I was excited about my birthday dinner with Ollie. Maybe it was because I never had much of a birthday before Ollie came into my life, but I really looked forward to them now. Ollie always found something different or fun to do. Last year it was zip lining in West Virginia, and my sophomore year it was a four-day cruise in the Caribbean. What would he think of this year?

The only thing I knew for certain was that we would go to Red Lobster. It was our tradition even though both of us had long ago lost interest in Red Lobster. During dinner Ollie handed me a small box and wished me happy birthday. I opened the paper and found the box was from a company called YourAncestor.com. Looking to Ollie for some explanation he said, "Remember last year when you started having a tremor in your hand and said you wished you knew more about your family health history? And remember all the times we talked about you not having a clue about your father's identity? Well, I was listening to this fellow on the radio and he talked about finding his ancestors through yourancestor.com. I don't know if it is for real or a party game, but I thought what the hell."

I can't say I was excited about the gift, but I did my best to show appreciation for it. Inside the box was a vial, instructions and padded envelope for sending the vial back to the company. I briefly read the info and got the gist of it. I was to deposit saliva in the vial and they would extract my DNA from it. In turn they could tell me my nationality and also identify any people that also did the saliva test that were genetically related to me. I think Ollie knew I wasn't too fired up about it and he told me just forget it. I of course said that I appreciated it and would be happy to send my spit their way.

The next day I was telling my roommates about yourancestor.com and they got all excited. One of them had read about it in the *National Enquirer* and that just about proved my theory that yourancestor.com is a hoax. Nevertheless, they coerced me into going through with the test. So I filled out the application including my email address, spit it the vial and mailed it. The instructions said it would take four to six weeks to get the results, and I thought, *Oh sure, I can just imagine.*

The Christmas break was for almost a month that year. I spent the time looking at graduate schools and studying for a couple of my tougher classes. I hadn't bothered to check my email during the break. Most all my communication with friends were through texting and I didn't even think of my email. The day before I was returning to school I decided to check email since the university used it as a way of communicating. I had lots of emails but most of them were junk. Then I saw one that was from yourancestor.com. *Well*, I thought, *this will be interesting. What will they even send me? Maybe it will be like a fortune cookie message, so generic that anyone could think it was them.*

When I opened it I first saw a graph that was labeled ethnicity estimate. It indicated that I was 47%Western European, 26% Scandinavian, 14% Ireland, 9% Great Britain and 4% other regions. Well, that didn't surprise me much because my mother had always told me she was French and German. Of course, did that mean my father's heritage was from Ireland and Scandinavia? That might explain my light complexion and blond hair. After thinking about it for a minute, I knew a couple of college professors who could tell me if it was even possible to get this information from just a little spit.

There was another whole category called DNA Matches. This section showed me other people who possibly matched my DNA. It said I had thirty-three 4th to 6th cousin matches. *Well*, I thought, *this should be interesting* and I clicked on the site. Indeed it had a list of names that were all codes and there were no email addresses. Apparently if I wanted to contact any of them I had to go through the yourancestor.com website. All of the names except one were 4-6th cousins. I got thinking about that and that meant my great-great-grandparent was a sibling to their great-great-grandparent. It all seemed pretty detached to me.

However, the first name on the list was different and it was identified as sweetsue2. It said the possible range was 1st or 2nd cousin and the reliability level was extremely high at 99%. Whoa, this meant I had a cousin out there in the world who also took the DNA test. First off, my mother was an only child. My mother would never tell me anything about my father, other than to say he was really smart and she didn't know if he had any siblings. I had always wondered about the origin of my first name. Delta is unusual and I thought it may have been a family name. One time when my mother was drunk she blurted out, "Hell, I named you Delta for that fraternity over on the Middle Ohio University campus. That's where you came from, so why shouldn't I call you that." I thought she was just trying to hurt me and never thought about it again.

Throughout the rest of the day I couldn't stop thinking about the information I received. What if I did have a cousin out there? Obviously the person is interested in genealogy otherwise they wouldn't have taken the test. Should I email them back or not? This was a time to call on old reliable Ollie. Throughout the years Ollie always provided a great listening ear. He always waited till I was through talking and only then did he ask a question. For an uneducated truck driver he was really street smart about lots of things. I knew I had to talk with him.

"Ollie, how you doing?" I asked.

"Fine," he replied.

"Where you at right now?" I said.

"I'm just outside Atlanta on 75. What's up?" he queried.

"Well, I have two pieces of news for you. First, I took the MCAT last Saturday for medical school. I think I did really well on it. The second piece of news is rather different. You remember the DNA test you gave me for my birthday? I just got the results back and it is really interesting. I'm 47% Western European, 24% Scandinavian and 14% Irish. But that is not the most interesting part. It came up with a match of someone it says is my 1st or 2nd cousin. What I wanted to ask you is, should I email this person back? Do you think it is legit?"

Ollie thought a moment and then said, "Well, the way I see it is what do you have to lose? You didn't think you had any relatives and if you were to find you had some that could be good or bad. You are twenty-two years old now and you can decide if and who you want as a relative. So just out of curiosity, you may want to check this out." We talked a while longer about regular things like when he was going to be home again and when I was heading back to school before we hung up.

For the next several days I thought about whether or not to send a message to my so-called cousin. The days turned into a week and I still hadn't decided what to do about it. Any indecision on my part stopped one evening when I opened my email to find a message from sweetsue2. The message was brief and said "Dear Sir or Madam: The kit you are managing under the name DA is a close match (1st or 2nd cousin) to my kit for sweetsue2 Would it be possible to get some ancestral information on DA?" So sweetsue2 must be really trying to find some ancestors. As if with my lack of family history, I could really help her—or at least I assumed it was a her.

I thought about it over the next couple of hours and then returned a message. "Dear sweetsue2: I would be glad to share ancestral information if I knew any. My mother died when I was fifteen and I never knew my father. My mother had no siblings, so if I had any cousins it would have to be from my father's side of the family. But, as I said, I don't know anything about him. Sorry, DA." I thought that would end it all. Sweetsue2 wanted to do something with her family tree and I was just a dead limb on the tree.

I was mistaken, because the next day I received another letter from sweetsue2. It said, "Dear DA: This is really interesting to me and sort of a mystery. I don't know how I could be a cousin on your father's side because my father only has one brother and that brother has two children both in their teens. Would you be willing to share your email address so that we can communicate more fully? My email is Sweetsue2@yahoo.com, waiting to hear from you, Sue."

"Dear sweetsue2: I personally think yourancestor.com messed up, but that being said I have no trouble giving you my email. Here it is. DA1993@gmail.com"

I didn't get another message or email for a few days and

then a rather long one came. "Dear DA: thanks for sharing your email. I don't think they messed up. Somehow we are cousins and I want to figure it out. I'll start by sharing some things about me to see if any of it rings a bell with you. My married name is Susan Blakely but my maiden name was Susan Ann Strong and I was born in Ann Arbor, Michigan in 1989. My father is Edward Strong and he is a financial advisor. My mother is Ann Fisher Strong and she was born in Minnesota. I have one younger brother Todd and he is getting his MBA at the Wharton School of Business. I am married to Thomas Blakely and we have two children, Peter age seven and Alison age five. I know both my parents' families have been in this country for generations. I think that is all for now. Bye, Sue."

My return email, "Sue: I am sorry but I couldn't find anything in the information you sent that rings a bell. The only thing of interest is that you were born in Ann Arbor and I am currently a student at U of M right now. My name is Delta Anderson and my mother's name was Holly Anderson. That is her maiden name since she was never married. Good luck in your search, Delta."

"Delta, you have a beautiful and also unusual name. I bet your mother was a fan of Tanya Tucker's song 'Delta Dawn.' I always thought my name was so boring, Sue. Anyway I looked through my genealogy records and couldn't find an Anderson in my family line. That means if we are cousins it definitely has to come from your father's side. Are you sure you don't have any information about him? Anything that could be a clue would help. I still live in the Ann Arbor area. Right now I am a stay at home mom but in a couple of years when the kids are a little older I am returning to my job as a loan originator at First Union Bank. Tom is a construction manager for Semco Developers and they specialize in medical center construction and remodeling. I am trying to share enough about me so you won't think I'm a nut case. What I am wondering is whether you would be comfortable meeting me for a cup of coffee so we can chat in person? Let me know, Sue."

"Sue, I don't see any harm in us meeting. I don't have any cousins so even if you are not my real cousin pretending you are would be okay for me. When I'm not in class or studying I work at the Starbucks on Washington 12 to 6 on Tuesday, Thursday and Sunday. What about meeting there at 6:00 p.m. next Tuesday? Let me know. Delta."

"Delta, I'll be there. Sue."

I was getting really excited about meeting with Sue. Maybe my excitement increased because two of my chemistry professors verified that the saliva test from yourancestor.com could identify DNA matches. They thought it was likely that we were cousins, maybe not just first cousins. Tuesday arrived and the excitement hadn't abated. The last hour of my shift I was looking at every customer entering the store but none of them established eye contact. Finally, five minutes before ending my shift my cousin came through the door. I say cousin because there wasn't a doubt in my mind that we were related.

The woman was tall, blonde, and fair-skinned. I felt like I was looking in a mirror. Since she'd had two kids her body was a little fuller than mine but even the shape of her face and her crooked smile looked similar to mine. Maybe I wanted this so bad that I was seeing things I wanted to see. My co-worker standing in front of the espresso machine called over to me and said, "Hey Delta, is that your sister that just came in the door?"

Sue must have had the same reaction, because she didn't look at anyone but me. I greeted her at the counter and called her by name. She reached across and grasped my hand as if to keep me from leaving. I noticed when she was reaching across the counter her hand was trembling just like mine does. Sue ordered a skinny sugar-free white chocolate latte, which happens to be my favorite drink too. When she tried to pay, I told her it was on me and if she would grab a seat I would make our drinks and be right over.

My mind was going a mile a minute. This situation was for real and she definitely was related to me. Would I finally learn who my father was and why he never wanted to meet me? What if he didn't want to meet me now? How would I handle being rejected by him again? So many things to think about and so little time to get myself put back together before sitting down with Sue. I carried her drink to the table using two hands and then went back to get my own drink. Sue said, "What was that all about? Why make two trips?" I chuckled and said, "I learned early on in this job to use two hands, otherwise there wouldn't be much drink left in the customer's cup."Then I held my hand out straight so that she could see the tremor. Sue then put her hand out almost touching mine and we both watched our hands shake.

We did the usual small talk about how nice it was to meet

in person, how much traffic there was on the road and how cold it has been. Then there was dead silence. It was like all the air had been sucked out of the room. Each of us was probably thinking the same thing, *What do I say next?* Sue broke the ice and said, "I see you've got the Strong Shakes too."

"Strong shakes?" I replied.

"Yeah, that's what we call them in our family. Lots of members of the Strong family have the same shake. It's called essential tremors and although not everyone in a family inherits it, it is genetically passed down from one generation to the next. My grandfather—whoops, I guess we can say your grandfather too—had the shakes really bad by the time he died. He had to drink everything through a straw or it would spill. My father has it, but Uncle Rob doesn't. However, my cousin, Uncle Rob's son, is only fifteen and already has the tremor."

I asked her what she thought when she saw me behind the counter. It was my way of checking to see if see had the same reaction. Sue said, "Once I laid eyes on you I knew I didn't have to ask where Delta was. We could pass for sisters. In fact, before I had babies I had your body shape. I'm 5'9" and would guess that you about the same height. Am I right?"

"Sue, I had the same reaction as you. In fact, one of my co-workers asked if you were my sister. And, yes I am a little over 5'9"."

We started talking non-stop about things we liked or didn't like. For example, I told her I wasn't like most women and didn't crave chocolate. I preferred fruit flavors and would always pick strawberry shortcake over a chocolate sundae any day. Neither of us cared for sports and never played on high school team, much to the chagrin of our respective basketball coaches. They both saw tall girls and couldn't believe neither of us had the coordination or interest to succeed in sports.

I told Sue about my life and didn't leave out any details. I told her about my mother's profession and the times I had been in foster care. She had a hard time understanding Ollie's role in my life, and as I tried to explain it I could see why. "Yes, I only met him the night before I asked if he would lie and say he was my uncle." It sounded outrageous even to me as I told it to her. By the time I finished talking about the things Ollie did for me and why I considered him my real father, Sue had tears in her eyes. All she could say to me was that I should write a book

Sue stated, "If we are cousins and not sisters, either Uncle Rob fathered you or my grandparents had another son they didn't tell me about."

She then dug in her purse and pulled out a stack of photos which she laid on the table. I picked them up and started looking at my people, people that I was genetically related too but didn't know. As I looked at the pictures she told me who was in each one. "Those are my children Peter and Alison; that's Tom, my husband, and me at a cottage we rented on Higgins Lake; there's the four of us at Disneyworld last year." I stared at each picture and could see I resembled her family. The next picture sent shivers down my spine. If I didn't know better, I would have thought it was a picture of me when I was twelve in a dance costume. Sue said, "That's Uncle Rob's daughter, Melissa when she was in dance."

I looked at Sue and said, "My God, she looks just like I did at that age."

Sue answered, "If that amazes you, wait till you see some of the others." She sorted through the pictures and picked out one of a teenage girl. "When I came in the door I thought I was looking at Melissa, only a few years older. I have no doubt that you are family and I only wish I could tell you how you are related, but I don't have the answer."

I continued looking at pictures and came to a large family group photo. Sue explained that it was her grandparents' 60th wedding anniversary and all the family was there. What caught my attention immediately was the man standing in the back row with a huge grin and his arms over the shoulder of Melissa and a boy that must be his son. I was looking at Rev. Rob Strong. Uncle Rob that Sue was talking about was the TV evangelist Rev. Rob. Then I thought, no way could Rev. Rob be my father. His whole message is the sanctity of the family and making moral decisions. All I could hear going through my head was his mantra, "Play the hand that was dealt you."

Sue didn't pick up on my discomfort and was pointing to individual family members and stating their name. When she took a breath I said, "Rev. Rob is your uncle? When you were talking about Uncle Rob I never thought that he was the famous TV preacher. Oh my God, do you think he's my father?"

Sue responded immediately, "Unless Nana and Gramps

had another boy they didn't tell anyone about, he would have to be your father. I can tell you right now that he wouldn't be too pleased finding out he had a daughter out there. Uncle Rob is just about set to run the for the open US Senate seat in Michigan. My father is taking time from his financial planning business to be Uncle Rob's campaign coordinator." Sue pointed to another man on the back row that looked very distinguished with gray hair and a Colgate smile and said, "That's my father, Edward." She took her time and identified all the people in the photo including my half-sister Melissa and half-brother Adam. The older couple sitting in the middle was my grandparents. She said, "Grandpa Strong died last year but Nana is still going strong at eighty-four years of age."

"What do I do now, Sue? There must be some reason why my existence has been such a secret. Who do you think we should talk to about it?"

"Delta, I need some time to process what has happened. Let's not do anything right now but take a step back and think through the situation. I can tell you that I am overjoyed in finding I have a new cousin. The stupid saliva tests have been the most exciting thing to happen to me in years. No matter how this turns out, rest assured you now have family—and that's me."

The first time we looked at the clock on the wall it was 8:30. We had been together two and a half hours and it felt like ten minutes, I think we both felt a bond had been established. The way we comfortably talked was different than the way I previously had talked with any friend. As we stood to say good night, Sue threw her arms around me and said, "Let's talk tomorrow and see if we can come up with the tack we should take."

Chapter 9

From that point on Sue and I talked or texted every day. We hadn't decided what should be done and that was okay with me. I had lived twenty-two years without my bio-father and there was no rush on my part to solve this entire puzzle since I now knew a lot of the pieces. My academic life was demanding my full attention. Whoever said the senior year was easy didn't major in Chemical Engineering at U of M. I felt buried and in many ways I was thankful that I was too preoccupied with school to deal with the paternity issue.

Over the next couple of months, Sue and Tom reached out to me in many ways and had me to their house in Northville several times for dinner. At first I felt uncomfortable about it, but that quickly lessened. I had never been in a family where people really seemed to love each other. Tom's relationship with his kids had me entranced. I guess I never thought that much about a father's role and the importance he played in the family. The second time I was to the house for dinner, Tom's brother Brady was there. Brady was in his mid-twenties, had been in the military, and now was a police officer in Plymouth. He had graduated from Eastern Michigan University with a degree in criminal justice and was currently attending law school at night at the University of Detroit.

I don't know if Sue intentionally planned to introduce Brady to me or it was a coincidence that he was there for dinner the same night. It was pretty obvious that we hit it off really well. Our conversation was so casual and relaxed. The only time it became tense was when he asked me what I was going to do about my father situation. I looked at Sue and she shrugged her shoulders and chuckled as she said, "Brady's not only family, but someone I love, and I don't keep secrets from family members that I love." Sue intimated that she grew up in a home that had lots of secrets and she didn't know why. She tried to explain it by saying her father's financial advising business was always hush-hush. Whenever the phone was for him he had to take it in the other room. She also said her mother had her own secrets such as her more than close relationship with the pastor at her church whom she saw for spiritual counseling. Sue calmly said, "I decided when I was an adult I wouldn't keep secrets from my family." I had never met a person that was as open and disclosing as Sue.

Before I left Sue's house, Brady asked for my phone number, and that started our practice of nightly phone calls. We talked for hours about all sorts of things like criminal justice, religion, the educational system, health care, and even family relations. The most difficult conversation we had was when he complained about arresting prostitutes because he thought it was a victimless crime. I got a little steamed when I told him how that victimless crime impacted me and let him know the children of prostitutes were often victims. I let him know I was such a victim. He took my outburst in stride and said he understood my point. Brady was a really deep guy and much more in tune with his feelings than I assumed a police officer would be.

Of course, I shared everything with Ollie. The man was my true north. In this instance, even the normally unflappable Ollie was surprised to find that Rev. Rob was possibly my birth father. True to form, no matter what the issue, questions were on target and somehow got me on the right track He didn't give me answers but asked questions that made me understand the situation better. Ollie said, "Delta, your mother was a prostitute which means she was having sexual relationships with lots of men. You are twenty-two, how old would Rev. Rob have been twenty-three years ago and where was he then? Didn't your mother make some joke about your name coming from a fraternity? Do you think she was giving you some kind of clue? Does this Sue Blakely think he is possibly your father?" The questions he posed helped me devise a strategy, which I was prepared to share with Sue.

BACK AT SUE'S HOUSE

Sue Blakely had been struggling with the same questions as Delta. How was it possible that Uncle Rob could be Delta's father? She thought about all the time she had spent with him; she knew him to be an honest and sincere man. She never bought into his evangelical approach to religion, but always believed that he was a true Christian. Sue had been raised in a more liberal mainstream theological environment than Rob's children. Her mother was very outspoken when it came to religion and encouraged Sue and her brother to think long and hard about their beliefs. She dragged Sue to a variety of churches over the years and after each church visitation asked Sue to tell her what she thought about the ideology of the church.

Through her email communication, phone calls, and many in-person meetings, Sue had developed a strong opinion about Delta. She saw Delta as extremely smart, but a self-protective and highly controlled individual. She thought Delta did not disclose about herself easily and probably had problems in her social relationships. At the same time, Sue hit it off really well with her. They connected from the very first contact. She didn't know if was genetic or just that their personalities matched, but she thought of Delta as a friend even more than a blood relative.

After Delta and Brady had left following the dinner on that second meeting and the kids were in bed, Sue and Tom sat on the sofa with their feet in each other's lap. As they massaged each other's feet, Sue started talking about the entire situation with Delta. She didn't keep anything from Tom so he knew how Sue was struggling with Delta's potential genetic relationship to Uncle Rob. At first he tried his best to find a flaw in the story and tear it apart. He just didn't see how it was possible that they were related, but after reading more about yourancestry.com and meeting Delta in person, he believed Delta could be Rob's daughter.

They talked about the three possible scenarios. First, was there a mistake in the testing? Tom said, "My God Sue she looks like she could be your sister and she looks even more like your cousin Melissa. It's spooky." They both agreed that she almost certainly was related. Sue continued, "Second, for her to be my cousin she has to be a child born to a child of my paternal grandparents. So is it possible that my grandparents had a son we know nothing about? Could this son have had a relationship with Delta's mother?" They both concluded that it is hard to keep secrets that big in a family. Someone in the extended family would have spilled the beans. So although possible, it was unlikely.

"What's behind door three, Johnny?" Sue joked. "My Uncle Rob has to be Delta's father and I find that so hard to believe. Uncle Rob is so straight I can't imagine him ever messing around on Aunt Michele. I know lots of men of the cloth and politicians are taken down by sex, but it is incomprehensible to me that Uncle Rob would be one of those men."

After some silence, Tom said, "Maybe he didn't cheat on Aunt Michele. How old is Delta?

"She just turned twenty-two, why?"

"How old would Uncle Rob have been twenty-two years ago and where was he at that time? Maybe we should consider twenty-three years ago too, since Delta's mother was pregnant for nine months before Delta was born. Also remember there are students who sell their sperm to donor banks for women using in vitro fertilization."

Sue answered, "I never thought about it from that angle, but Uncle Rob's conservative religious views probably would have made that a no-no for him. A far as history goes, Uncle Rob and Aunt Michele just celebrated their 20th anniversary. It was a big affair and we went to the party, remember. Off the top of my head I don't know where he was twenty-three years ago, but I can find out on Wikipedia."

Their heads were almost touching as Sue did a Google

search for Rev. Rob Strong. There were numerous sites to pick, but they chose Wikipedia because it was concise, although the information wasn't always accurate. "Uncle Rob is forty-four years old, so let's check his history and see what comes up." It was right in front of their eyes. Twenty-two years ago he was attending Cornerstone University in Grand Rapids, Michigan and he was there for three years obtaining a second bachelor's degree in Ministry Leadership and a master's degree in Business Administration. Twenty-three years ago he was a senior at Middle Ohio University getting a bachelor's degree in psychology.

They continued to read his impressive curriculum vitae that highlighted his successful ministry, including becoming one of the most popular television evangelists. Uncle Rob was a featured speaker around the nation and often talked to packed stadiums. He had written six books and currently had one on the New York Times Bestsellers List. His most recent venture has been in politics and his name was always bantered around as a possible candidate for governor or senator. Some people even thought there was a presidency in his future. Because of her father's involvement in the campaign, Sue knew he was running for US Senate.

Sue, Tom, and the kids had always enjoyed spending time with Uncle Rob. He was a fun guy that loved playing games. At family gatherings he was always the one to organize a football or softball game. Sue remembers as a child Uncle Rob always took Todd and her on camping trips. She found that most people liked him even if they didn't agree with his theology or politics. She and Todd were just like the majority of people. They liked Uncle Rob, just not necessarily his religious or political views. Most times Rob kept his views in check at family gatherings, but on several occasions he was over the top, particularly when he learned that Sue and Tom were living together before they were married. They felt the fire and brimstone coming from him as he lectured them on family values.

Sue thought about how Uncle Rob was so different from her father. The two Strong brothers couldn't be less alike. Edward was a numbers guy. He had his nose buried in financial worksheets. He couldn't have cared less about any other activities and was quite willing to have Rob take his kids on the typical family adventures. Sue wondered how her mother dealt with it, because they never did things as a family or socialized with friends. Maybe that's why she sought counseling with her pastor? Their social life, what there was of it, existed for Edward to solidify business and financial contacts. However, Edward was well known in his own right as the financial advisor for some extremely powerful and wealthy people.

Rob, on the other hand, was the empathic one. He made everyone he came into contact with feel as if they were the most important people when he talked with them. He made friends easily and could influence others through his talks. The last couple of years Uncle Rob had very little time to himself and had left the church he built in Okemos called the People's Tabernacle to focus more on his television show and writing. In spite of his busy schedule he found time for his family. Sue had spent lots of time with Melissa and Adam, her cousins, and to her they seemed like pretty normal teenagers.

"Tom, I think I am going to talk with my father about this situation and get his advice."

"It's your decision, Sue, but I'd be careful how you approach your dad with your uncle's campaign coming up."

Chapter 10

"Brady, you've been in a daze this whole shift. What's going on with you today?" said Patrolman Mark Lindsey. Mark had been Brady's partner since he joined the force three years ago, and they knew each other very well. They were both about the same age, single, and very interested in their law enforcement career. Recently, along with going to law school at night, Brady had been studying with Mark for the sergeant's exam.

Brady knew what was bothering him. There was a new woman is his life and she was on his mind constantly. He was staying up beyond his normal bedtime just so he could talk to her. How soon he forgot that college students live on a completely different time cycle than the rest of the world. He thought back to his time in college and remembered that only freshmen got early-morning classes. Upper classmen made sure they didn't start class till 10:00 a.m., at the earliest. Heck, he didn't even think about going out at night till 11:00 p.m. So the only time to catch Delta was late at night.

Brady loved talking with Delta. He had never met a girl like her. She was really book smart but another side of her was really naïve. There were some things she shared easily about her life but some things she seemed to be holding back. Brady knew that her adoptive father was a truck driver and her mother was deceased, but generally she held back other information. If Sue hadn't told him about the DNA test, he bet Delta would have let him believe that the truck driver was her biological father.

He found that Delta was a great conversationalist if it wasn't too personal. She could talk all day about the educational system or whether God was dead or alive, but ask about how she felt about her mother's death and she clammed up. Brady loved a challenge and Delta was a formidable one.

The next step in their relationship was a date. He had been with Delta in person only at his brother's house for dinner, and all the rest of the contact was by phone. Asking her for a date was going to be tricky. Sue seemed really protective of Delta and he didn't know if Sue was in agreement with his dating her. To preserve the relationship with Sue and also not put his brother on the spot, Brady decided to ask Sue for permission before asking Delta out.

After his shift the next day, he decided to drop in on Tom and Sue. This was not unusual because Brady really loved being with his niece and nephew. He often came by the house just to spend time with them. Brady spent some time in the back yard with the kids and then gravitated to the kitchen where Sue was preparing supper. After pulling a beer from the fridge, Brady sat on a stool by the island and looked at Sue. She spoke first. "Okay, what do you want? I know that look and can tell you want something."

Brady waited a minute and then said, "Sue, what do you think about me dating Delta?"

Sue responded, "You only met her at that one dinner—what makes you think you want to date her?"

"Delta and I have been talking on the phone every day for the past three weeks. I think I know her pretty well but at the same time I know your relationship with her is highly unusual and I don't want to create a problem for either of you."

"I appreciate you talking with me about it, and I don't have a good answer. You know that Delta and I are cousins and we suspect my Uncle Rob is her biological father. I need to talk to my father about the situation but I have been holding back. I feel like I may be opening Pandora's Box. On the other hand, I really like Delta and know that she needs some resolution to the situation. Would you mind holding off for a little while till I talk with my father about it?"

"Of course not, Sue, just let me know when you think the time is right. I just know that personally I am really attracted to Delta and would like to see where the relationship goes."

Brady called Delta that same evening and decided to tell her what he had discussed with Sue. In one way he wanted Delta to know that he wanted to ask her out, but he also wanted to let her know that he respected Sue's request. Delta seemed to take it all in stride. She let him know that dating was perfectly agreeable with her, but she was also buried with school work. She had a few weeks of school left before graduation and she also was putting together all her applications for medical schools.

After a little dead air on the phone Delta said, "Brady, I just love talking to you each night. In many ways I feel like it has brought both of us really close. But I can wait a while before we date if that's okay with you?"

Over the next few weeks, Brady poured all his energy into studying for the sergeant's exam. Plymouth was a nice little city north of Detroit and didn't have many of the big-city issues. He was really happy to be on their police force and could see himself moving up the ranks. Most of the serious crime in Plymouth was a result of being close to Detroit. He responded to a lot of B & E's and drug sales, but most times he was busy with traffic violations and domestic disputes.

Checking the mail when he got home from work, there was a square envelope with his name and address handwritten on it. The mail he usually received were bills from credit card companies, gas, cable, and stuff like that. He didn't recognize the Ann Arbor return address on the envelope and thought maybe it was a wedding announcement from one of his friends or relatives. As he opened the letter he saw that it was an invitation to Delta's open house in celebration of her graduation.

Brady called Delta as soon as he received the invitation and told her that he would be there. Delta told him that she was nervous sending it to him because she thought he might think she was too forward, but her father had forced the issue. Her father said that they were going to have a party and he was renting a room near Ann Arbor for it. Delta said that he thought that if they had it at their house in Greenville, not many would show up. She hated to tell him that she had so few friends that not many would show up anyway.

When she told Brady about her father's push to have a party, she made the mistake of saying that she was scrounging for anyone she knew to invite to the party. Brady challenged her and said, "You mean the only reason I'm invited is to have people there?" When Delta told him she could have died from embarrassment, he burst into laughter. He assured her that he was coming regardless of her attitude.

Delta couldn't keep Brady off her mind and was so surprised that he wanted to come to her open house. She was so taken back that on a whim She said, "Brady, would you also like to come to my graduation ceremony? It is probably boring and you don't have to but I have four tickets and so far my father is the only one using a ticket."

Conversation about the graduation tickets catapulted quickly and by the next day Sue and Tom had claimed the last two tickets. This was going to be interesting. Ollie was going to meet her newly found cousin, her husband, and brother-in-law for the first time, and she wasn't going to be there to assist because she would be waiting for her diploma.

Graduation at a big university was not like anything she had expected. Since there were so many students each college had their own graduation ceremony. This made the event manageable and the engineering school had only a couple of hundred graduates including masters and doctoral students, but it still had all the pomp and circumstance plus.

Ollie made sure Delta had the full packet of graduation photos and he presented her with a bouquet of roses before the event. If she didn't know better, she would have thought that Ollie was graduating too. Delta had a chance to introduce Sue, Tom, and Brady to Ollie earlier in the day, and She then watched his eyes twinkle when she said, "I'd like you to meet my father." If she had any concerns about the four of them getting along, they quickly dissipated. Ollie became the host and greeted them all like they were long- lost friends.

Delta didn't have a clue what the four of them were talking about in the auditorium. All she knew is that at the end of the ceremony they were all laughing and treating each other like friends. She also couldn't believe that Ollie found a Red Lobster that had a meeting room for her party but he found one in Chelsea, which wasn't too far away. Delta was shocked when she saw over twenty people there. Her college roommates, two professors, a bunch of people from Starbucks, and even two of her friends from Greenville made the trip up.

The party was perfect and she couldn't have been happier. Nothing like this had ever happened to her before and it looked as if she could get used to it. Ollie was the proud father and made sure everyone's needs were met. When they were all seated Ollie stood up and said, "I would like to offer a toast. I would like everyone to raise their glass. Not one of you knows Delta's and my history. If I told you about it, you would think I had made up a story. However, I want to toast my beautiful, smart daughter who has gone through more in her brief lifetime than you would ever believe. She never let adverse conditions interfere with her striving for success and always kept a positive attitude. As her father, I couldn't be prouder of her accomplishments, but I have to tell you that regardless of her accomplishments it's her character that I love. I never thought

I could love anyone like I love Delta and I am so glad that she is part of my life."

Tears were flowing down both their cheeks. Delta was sure the other guests thought it was just a dad spouting off about his daughter. She knew different. She knew that their relationship that initially was built on her need for a guardian had grown into real love. Delta stood up and hugged Ollie and then indicated that she wanted to speak too. She looked around the room and realized that the only people that knew her story besides Ollie were Sue, Tom and Brady. Delta began, "As my father said, you don't know our history but I can share this with you. Oliver Kendall Jordan III came into my life when I was the most vulnerable. My mother had just died and I had nobody and I mean nobody. Ollie was a complete stranger to me, yet he stepped up and became my guardian. He adopted me when I turned eighteen and has been the one sure thing I have ever known in my life."

The room was silent when she turned to Ollie and said, "Dad, you have done so much for me that I could never repay. You have been there for me every day even when it meant you had to give up something for yourself." Delta reached for her purse and took out an envelope. Looking at Ollie she said, "Dad, I want one more thing from you if you are okay with it."

She handed him the envelope, which he opened and read carefully. Then he looked at her and said, "Yes, of course, yes." While he was hugging her Delta announced to the guests that she had legally changed her last name from Anderson to Jordan in honor of her father. There wasn't a dry eye in the house.

After everyone had left, Delta told Ollie that she started the process to legally change her name a few months ago. She realized that identifying her birth father through DNA only proved to her that her attachment was to Ollie and not some sperm donor. All of her graduate school applications had Jordan as the last name, and she had the university make the change on their records.

By 9:00 p.m., Ollie had got on the road back to Greenville and everyone had left except Brady. Throughout the open house, Brady made his presence known. He introduced himself to Delta's friends and seemed to be genuinely glad to be there. Brady ended up spending most of the time with Ollie. He had completed a tour in Afghanistan after going to Eastern Michigan, and he was an M.P. in the Army, which improved his chances of getting a job in law enforcement. So the two men had lots to talk about. Brady had shared a bit of his military experience with Delta during their long evening phone conversations and she knew he carried a heavy burden from some of experiences in Afghanistan.

Brady walked Delta out the door and even though she said it was silly he said that he would follow her home to make sure she got there safely. He walked her to the front door and took both her hands in his. He looked her in the eye and told her what a nice day it had been. It almost seemed old-fashioned when he said, "Delta, would you consider going out on a date with me?"

She sort of chuckled, which made him blush. "Brady," she said, "as I told you before, we have talked on the phone every day for hours. Do you think I would talk to someone if I wasn't interested in getting to know them better?"

"I guess that means yes?" he said and then he pulled her closer and pressed his lips to hers at first in a brotherly way. She broke the hand hold and put her hands on his shoulders so she could pull him closer to her. She pulled his head toward her and really gave him a kiss. She parted his lips and ran her tongue over his bottom lip. He didn't hesitate to match his tongue with hers and both their temperatures rose quickly. Before it got too involved she ended the kiss and thanked him for seeing her home.

As he got to the sidewalk he turned to her and said, "Oh, just so it's all above board, I have asked Sue if it was all right to date her cousin."

When he first told her he was asking Sue, she was taken back with the idea that he asked someone's permission, but now for the first time she felt connected to Sue as a relative. This sudden realization that she had a relative that cared for her was a feeling that would take some getting used to. Sue was looking out for Delta's best interests and Brady respected her for it. Delta thought, *life was never complicated by relatives in the past, but things had changed and I'd better get used to it.*

Chapter 11

When Brady arrived back at his apartment he was acutely aware that he didn't remember anything that happen on the ride home. He must have been on auto pilot, and as a police officer that was not acceptable. Brady's only thought was about the kiss from Delta and how it hit him like a lightning bolt. Her lips were so soft and when her tongue spread his lips, it felt like velvet. She was unlike any girl he had ever dated. Delta was a mixture of sophistication, complexity, intelligence, inexperience, and simplicity.

Brady knew bits and pieces of her life, but not the whole story, and that was something he wanted to know. As much as he enjoyed talking with Ollie, it was clear that he wasn't going to talk about Delta's past. He knew that her mother died when she was fifteen, her father was probably Rob Strong, and her adopted father met her when her mother died. He didn't have much information about a girl that was occupying his mind almost all the time. It was clear that their backgrounds were totally different, and yet they really connected with one another.

Brady thought about his own family and what a normal childhood he had. Tom and he had grown up in a family that would have made the Cleavers envious. His dad was an engineer for Chrysler and must have made good money, because money was never discussed at home. His mother taught school before she had children and then was a stay-at-home mother once she had children. She was home every day when he got out of school and she attended all his school activities. They lived in a small town in Oakland County called Clarkston that was like stepping back in the past. Kids could ride their bikes downtown and neighbors knew each other. About the only crime they experienced were driving violations, or destruction of mailboxes with baseball bats.

Tom was the smart one in the family and aced all his classes. Brady followed a couple of years behind Tom and was just an average student. However, Brady was the jock in the family, and that gave him lots of recognition. Brady played football, hockey, and baseball, but his favorite sport was hockey. By the time he was a senior in high school, a couple of college hockey teams were interested in him, but that all came to an end when he fractured his ankle snowboarding during winter break of his senior year.

Brady learned at a young age that it was important to help others, particularly those less fortunate than himself. His parents were big into volunteering and expected the same of their children. As a family, they worked the food bank and served meals once a month at the Salvation Army Shelter. They participated in park clean-ups, parades, flower planting, and any number of civic duties to improve their community. As an adult, Brady still felt it was his responsibility to help others and his choice of a career in law enforcement reflected that. He didn't go into law enforcement to stop crime per se; Brady wanted to help people who were affected by crime.

Brady went to Eastern Michigan University because he

couldn't get accepted at Michigan. He always thought he had a good education there and found he really enjoyed his major in criminal justice. One professor had a lot of influence with Brady, and it was this person who encouraged him to enlist in the military. The professor said that he would have an easier time getting a job in law enforcement coming out of the military, and besides it would be a good experience for him.

In hindsight, the professor was correct about getting the job in law enforcement. With his degree in criminal justice and his experience as a military police officer, Brady had his pick of a few police departments. He chose Plymouth because it was large enough to offer the opportunity of advancement, but small enough that he wouldn't get lost.

However, he didn't come away from the military experience in good shape. At first, being in the service was like being on a sports team. The spirit and attitude were infectious. Toward the end of his tour, he had an experience that still gave him bad dreams. His team had identified a pocket of insurgents and called in for air support. There must have been a mistake on the coordinates, because the air support hit a school that was in session. Brady could still smell the burning flesh and the image of the surviving children trying to get out of the building was clear in his mind.

When it came time to re-up, Brady chose to go home. His parents were thrilled with his decision, since they had never encouraged him to enlist in the first place. By the time he accepted the job with the Plymouth Police Department Tom and Sue had already started their family. Maybe it was his experience in Afghanistan or maybe just his maturity, but he loved being with happy children, particularly his niece and nephew. He probably was a pest to his sister-in-law since he was at their house as often as possible, just because he couldn't get enough of the kids.

Brady's parents never pushed him to talk about his war experience, but they knew he had been damaged. Likewise, they never asked why he didn't have a steady girlfriend although they thought someone in their late twenties should start to settle down. His parents loved the idea of family and assumed that their kids would be just like them and be happily married. What would his parents think if he brought Delta home? Her life experiences were so different from theirs. Could Delta even begin to understand how they felt about family? They took Sue into their home as if she were their daughter, but even with her he had heard them talking about Sue's family as being cold and uncaring. Would they even begin to understand the life that Delta had lived?

Early the next morning Brady sent a text message to Delta stating: "Hey Delta, I have tickets for the Maroon 5 at Pine Knob on Saturday. Would you like to go with me? Please say yes. Brady"

Delta responded, "I love Maroon 5. Count me in. What time?"

Brady picked her up at 6:30 p.m. and the date was perfect. The band was incredible and the weather was great. Brady had packed a bottle of wine and a variety of deli containers he picked up at Trader Joe's. They stretched out on the blanket and absorbed everything going on around them. The night was magical and by the end of the evening neither he nor Delta wanted the night to end.

Brady walked her to her door after the concert, thinking of ways to extend the night. Delta picked up on his thoughts and said, "Would you like to come in?" Her roommates had already left for the summer, so they had the house to themselves. Delta got a couple of cold beers out of the fridge and put some popcorn in the microwave. By the time she returned to the living room Brady was curled up on the sofa watching the late, late show. Delta handed him a beer and put the popcorn between them.

They both lost interest in the television as Brady put his arms around her and pulled her close. They stayed in that position for the next couple of hours and shared stories about their life experiences. Every once in a while Brady would nuzzle Delta's neck or stroke her arms, but he never ventured beyond cuddling.

Chapter 12

Maybe it was having Brady's arms around me and feeling the warmth of his body that gave me a great sense of security. I shared things that I had never shared with anyone else. I told him about all the times my mother had made promises and didn't follow through. I talked about my life living with a drug- and alcohol-addicted prostitute. I talked about the times in school when I was ostracized because of the way I dressed and where I lived, including the horrible time I had at the one birthday party I was invited to. As I was talking, tears were flowing down my cheeks. I don't think I ever grieved for my loss of a childhood, and that was happening now.

Probably what surprised me the most was being able to tell Brady about being sexually molested and raped in foster care. I had never even told Ollie everything that happened to me in foster care. I knew Ollie put two and two together and figured out most of what happened to me. What I appreciated the most about Brady was that he took off his policeman's hat and didn't ask questions. He let me talk, and talk I did.

The only time Brady asked a question was when I talked about Ollie. I think he was trying to figure out if Ollie was for real and what was in it for him. I told Brady the true story and how the protective services worker went along with our deception. Most of all I didn't hold back about my feelings for the man. "Ollie gave me a reason to hope and helped me trust in people again. I couldn't love him more if me were my birth father and I know he feels the same toward me. So if you plan to be around me, you have to accept the fact that Ollie is part of the package."

Brady looked me in the eye and said, "I plan to be with you for a long time. You are really special and in the short time we've known each other I can honestly say I haven't felt this way about anyone else before." With that statement he looked at his watch and saw that it was 3:00 a.m. Pulling me into his arms he gave me a kiss that made my knees weak. I could have stayed in his arms for hours but he ended the kiss and said, "Remember where we left off, okay?"

It took me a little while to get to sleep, as my thoughts were going in double time. How could I be falling for a guy at this time? He just started his law enforcement career in Plymouth and I had my heart set on going to medical school at Johns Hopkins University all the way out in Baltimore. Why was I even considering Brady at this time? I never thought about my future with a guy in it. It wasn't that I was opposed to a long-term relationship or even marriage, but I never considered it. Now I was even thinking about other medical schools that had a strong research component like the new campus Michigan State started in Grand Rapids, or just staying at Michigan. I already had received acceptance letters at both those medical schools.

I thought spending the money for applications to more than one school was wasteful but Ollie wouldn't hear of it and he provided about $12,000 just for the MCAT and the application fees. The lowest school application fee was $3,000 and the most expensive was $4,200. I got into the schools I applied for and couldn't imagine how I would have felt if I was rejected. Someday if I have time I was going to do a complete research project why medical schools cost so much. I looked at the clock and it said 3:50. That was the last thing I remembered

I was still on school time and woke up at 8:00 with my eyes wide open. After making a cup of coffee I was anxious to call Sue. She had become a really good friend and was more than interested in my date with her brother-in-law. She must have checked her caller ID, because as soon as it rang she said, "Finally you call. I have been going crazy waiting to hear from you. You have to tell me everything and don't leave a thing out."

"Hello to you too," I said.

Sue responded, "No, wait, I have a better idea. Why don't you come over to my house and spend the day with me? I was planning on going to Eastern Market to stock up on veggies and fruit. Then we can go to the Russell Street Deli for one of their great omelets.. We can do the girlfriend thing and make a day of it. What do you say?"

I thought for a minute and realized I always had an excuse for not spontaneously going out when invited. I would say I was too busy, had to work, and had to study. I no longer had any excuse— and besides, I really enjoyed Sue's company. I answered, "All right, Sue, that sounds great. I do have to tell you that I may be the only person in the greater Detroit area that has never been to Eastern Market."

Sue chuckled. "Oh, my gosh, I didn't realize what a sheltered life you've led. Well, girlfriend, get over here so we can be on the road by 9:30. You are going to think you are in a foreign country. The sounds and smells alone will do that but wait to you see the produce, cheese, and meat. Oops—I almost forgot about the flowers. They are just beautiful too."

I arrived at Sue's house a little before 9:30 with two coffees with extra sugars and cream from Biggby's coffee. I could see she was in the process of putting a wagon with wooden rail sides in the back of her van. She also put a stack of cloth shopping bags and bungee straps in with the wagon. Sue said, "You'd never survive shopping at Eastern Market if you tried to carry all the items. The cart makes all the difference in the world. Would you believe Tom gave this to me for Christmas two years ago just so I could use it at the market? Everyone thought he had bought it for the kids. Well, climb on in my soccer mom's car and let's hit the road."

The trip to Eastern Market was great. The market was huge and there was just a special feeling being in the market. I had never shopped for more than two people and couldn't believe what Sue was buying for a family of four. As a stay-at-home mom she prepared meals every breakfast and at night. She also packed a lunch for the kids each school day. The few years Ollie and I lived together I bought groceries once a week and only needed two or three bags to cover us for the week.

Sue led me to the Russell Street Deli, which already had a line at 11:30 a.m. Since we were too late for omelets, she suggested that I try the corned beef sandwich, but after looking at the menu I picked the grilled vegetarian sandwich. It was fantastic. This day was turning out to be really special, and different than what I had experienced before on shopping days. The best part was that Sue and I were really connected. We knew we were cousins by blood, but more important, we were becoming close friends.

While we were having lunch I told Sue about my date with Brady. I didn't leave anything out. I told her how romantic the night at Pine Knob had been picnicking on the blanket and then being under the stars while listening to a concert. I also told her about our long talk back at my apartment, and with some urging I told her about the two magical kisses we had shared. Sue knew I was headed to medical school and just listened as I struggled, telling her my dilemma about going to school out east.

Following lunch, we walked to Mootown Creamery and each of us ordered a shake to go. As we walked Sue said, "I have decided to tell my father about us. It seems like the logical thing to do. He'll know how to approach Uncle Rob, particularly since he is playing such a big role in his election campaign. Are you comfortable with my telling him?"

I didn't know if I was comfortable or not. The whole situation was so unusual I couldn't think of a right or wrong approach. I really wasn't looking for a father. I had a father, even if it was finding him late in my life. What did I expect to happen? Did I think Rev. Rob would come running and throw his arms around me? Did he even know I existed? All these thoughts were floating through my mind.

I told Sue, "Yeah, I guess it makes sense for you to talk with your father. I just want you to know that I am not expecting anything from him and I don't want him to think I am after money or stuff like that."

We made it back to Sue's house in time for the Peter and Alison to be dropped off by the school bus. One thing I liked about Sue was that she wanted her kids to learn about life. She complained about all the parents that drop off and pick up their kids each day. Sue told me that there was a lot to be learned by riding the bus. Oh, did I know the truth in that statement. Her children had met me a couple of times and Sue had told them to call me Aunt Delta. She said that it would be too hard trying to explain our cousin relationship, and that my age was perfect to be an aunt.

Sue told the kids to go into the house, drop off their backpacks, and put on some play clothes. Even Alison at age five had no trouble following her directions. Sue was doing something right with her kids. Before they ran to the house they each gave me a hug and said goodbye. I told Sue I was moving back to Greenville for the summer and double checked to be sure she had my address. I knew she had my cell phone number since no one has a home phone these days. Sue threw her arms around me and gave me a huge hug while telling me I had better keep in touch or she would have to drive down to Greenville.

Hugs were something I wasn't used to, and I guess if I was going to be around Sue and her family I better get used to it. I was never hugged as a child and even with Ollie our hugs were few and far between. The first time Sue hugged me, I froze. I am sure she thought she was hugging a tree. I consciously made an effort to improve my hugs. Boy, that sounds strange to say, even though I was the one thinking it. I realized when Sue or the kids came to hug me I drew in a deep breath and tightened all my muscles. I found help when I Googled "giving a great hug." It suggested to hug like you mean it, try to match the breath of the person you are hugging, close your eyes and lean into the embrace, but do not squeeze too hard.

As I read further I realized why hugging was difficult for me. It said that to hug was making yourself vulnerable. It is letting a person know that you trust them and are allowing them into your personal space. In order to survive as a child, I had to protect my personal space and there was no one I really trusted. I'm not sure if I can ever learn to hug as comfortably as Sue, but at least now I understood what I was up against.

Chapter 13

Sue was excited to tell Tom about her day with Delta. She was like a kid who met a new friend and couldn't wait to tell her mother about her surprise new friend and cousin. Tom listened and smiled as she talked. He said, "I am not surprised that you get along so well with her. If I didn't know better, she could be your sister. Right from the first time I met her, she seemed to have a personality that would mesh well with yours."

Sue told him that she was going to share all the information about Delta tomorrow with her father. The fact that Tom didn't say much was in reality saying a lot. She knew that her father was a very intense person who didn't display much affection or feelings toward others. He was a good provider, but that was the extent of his fatherly duties. Sue often wondered how and why her mother tolerated him all these years. But that being said, Sue knew he was an analytical type and would think things through before acting on them. She was certain that he would be very careful before approaching Uncle Rob.

Sue called him at his office the next day. His first response to her call was to ask if everything was okay. Sue never called him at the office. She learned when she was very young that Daddy did not want family interfering with work. She reassured him that things were okay, but that she needed to talk with him in person. His immediate reply was for Sue to come to their house tonight. He would be home about 7:30 p.m.

Sue waited a second before she responded and then said, "Dad, I want to discuss something with just you and I think it is best that we meet at your office." He tried to talk her out of it and also tried to get her to tell him the issue.

When he saw that it was a losing cause he said, "Fine, if you need to see me alone and don't want the kids or Tom present, then come to my office at 7:00 tonight. Will that work for you?"

Sue told him that was perfect and she would be there on time. Her father was a stickler for timeliness and she didn't want to get started on the wrong foot. Throughout the rest of the day Sue rehearsed in her mind what she was going to say. She also made copies of the DNA report for herself and Delta and before the kids got home from school she poured herself a rather large glass of merlot. Trying to relax was a challenge when she knew that what she revealed would shake up her rather mundane family. What she was going to tell her father was something you read about in novels, not in a real life.

Her father's office was located in an upscale office building off of I-275 in Livonia. He had been in a few different office buildings during her lifetime and was always willing to move to a new location as he always wanted to be in a building that smelled of success. He often said that his customers want to know he is a success because if he isn't a success, how could he make them financially successful? Sue had never been to his latest office but even she was surprised by its opulence. It was a two-story modern structure with exquisite landscaping and exterior lighting. Even at 7:00 at night there was a guard inside the door at a receptionist's counter. The building had several offices all serviced by the main foyer. There was the wealth management office for a local bank, two attorney's offices, and another private investment firm.

The foyer was huge with a large salt water tank stretching about twenty feet across the back wall. The bronze signs identified the various offices but did not direct you where to go. It was clear if you didn't know where to go, you shouldn't be there. The security guard immediately addressed her and asked what office she was looking for. After Sue told him, he asked her to sign the log sheet which identified her, time of day, who she was visiting and the last space was for the time she left.

The guard directed her down a hallway and told her Edward P. Strong & Associates' office was the second door on the right. When she reached the door there was a discreet sign telling her she was at the right office. Sue opened the door and walked into another luxurious space. The furniture was sleek and modern and another large salt water tank with all the colorful fish adorned the side wall. There was also a seating area facing a large flat screen TV still turned on to Bloomberg news. The receptionist's desk was vacant, so she thought it was safe to call out his name. "Dad, are you here?" She listened a while and called again, "Dad."

From a distance she heard his voice saying, "I'm coming."

Sue started walking toward the voice when an attractive woman came toward her, still straightening out her skirt. As

Sue got closer, she could see that this woman could easily be a model. The woman immediately called Sue by name and introduced herself as Angela Morales, administrative assistant to her father. She led Sue back to an office where her father was sitting behind a large mahogany desk. He said, "I see you have met Angela." He then turned to Angela and said, "I don't think there is any reason for you to hang around tonight. So why don't you close up—and be sure to lock the door on the way out."

After Angela left, he asked Sue if she needed a drink, because he was going to have one. Her father walked over to full panel sliding door which exposed a complete wet bar. Every top-shelf liquor was on display on the shelves above the bar. She could also see a sink and refrigerator, making the bar complete. He poured himself about three fingers of Glenlivet 21-year-old scotch, and told her that he had water and soft drinks. Sue decided to keep it simple and said she would have the same as him.

Edward moved over to a seating area and set both drinks down on engraved leather coasters that said Edward P. Strong & Associates. Sue sat down across from him and said, "I thought your last office was spectacular, but this one is over the top."

He nodded in agreement and added, "I can't tell you how much new business we brought in after moving here—and I mean people who are the real deal. Anyway, enough talk about the office; what is so important that you had to come here to talk about it?"

Sue took a deep breath and started, "I don't know if you

remember, but when Alison and Peter were born I did some family research so see if there were family first names that appealed to me. In fact, I found both of their names were also names of several of our ancestors. Since that time I have developed an interest in genealogy and have a family tree for my kids that show our family as well as Tom's family histories. I have really enjoyed doing the searches and communicating with other people also interested in the same ancestor as me. Some of my best information came from other people. For example, I was struggling with the Strong line and by talking with another researcher who shared the same grandparent as us I found John Strong who settled in Hingham, Massachusetts in 1635. John is your 9th great-grandfather and my 10th great-grandfather."

"I got so excited I even went online and visited the Old Ship Church cemetery in Hingham and made a copy of his tombstone. Did you know Hingham is close to Plymouth? I am trying to find a relative that came over on the Mayflower—but no luck so far."

Edward sat quietly listening and not interrupting. He was a master at listening and very good at knowing your intentions before you shared them. His years as a financial advisor had fine-tuned these skills. Sue knew she had to get to the heart of the situation soon.

She continued, "Dad, a genealogy company I use has a service that checks your DNA and matches it to other people who share your DNA. It cost less than $100, and I decided to do it a couple of years ago. The results told me that I was 44% English, 20% Irish, and 30% Western European, which didn't surprise me. The part that was interesting was the DNA matches. It listed over sixty people that were my 4th to 6th cousins, and then a year ago a new name was added. It said this person was my 1st or 2nd cousin with 99% reliability. "

"I didn't know who this person could be, since I know my two first cousins. The company has their own confidential communication system to use if you want to contact that person. I decided to use the ID assigned by yourancestor.com to make contact with this cousin and got a return message. The woman that replied said that she didn't have any cousins on her maternal side and therefore if we were related it had to be on her father's side. The real interesting thing is that she had no clue as to her father's identity. We exchanged email addresses and started communicating on a regular basis."

"Let me interrupt you right here," said her father. "You have taken a major risk. There are scam artists working the internet every day. You wouldn't believe what I have to pay a HTM Data Security to keep my financial records protected. You have exposed yourself—and who knows, maybe our whole family—in a dangerous way. I'm going to notify my company right away and get to the bottom of this."

As soon as he took a breath Sue said, "You're going to be really unhappy then with the rest of the stuff I am going to tell you. I have met this woman several times. She has been to the house for dinner; I attended her graduation and have gone shopping with her. Let me show you this and see if it changes your mind."

Sue got out her phone and showed him a couple of selfies

she took with Delta at Eastern Market. They looked like sisters out for a good time.

Edward looked at the picture and said, "This is just the kind of thing scam artists do. They find people that look alike and try to convince you they are family. Next thing you know she'll be asking for money—or worse yet if you left her alone in the house, she probably already has your computer hacked."

Sue took two pages from a folder and laid them in front of her father. She showed him the DNA report for Delta and herself. She gave him a brief introduction to how the service got the DNA and then showed him on her laptop how many people shared some of her DNA.

"Dad," she said, "I am convinced Delta is my cousin. She didn't seek me out and only did the DNA test at the urging of her adoptive father. She just graduated summa cum laude from the University of Michigan with a BS in chemical engineering. She has been accepted to four prestigious medical schools and will be attending one of them in the fall. Even though I have only known her for the last several months, I like and trust her. Her mother had no siblings, so the relationship has to be through the paternal side. That means Uncle Rob is her father, or else Grandma or Grandpa had a baby boy we didn't know about."

"That's enough, Sue," her father said sharply. "If you think for a minute that Uncle Rob fathered a child I don't know about, then you are out of your mind. These accusations have gone far enough and I want—no, I demand—that you cease all further contact with this person. Don't you realize that Uncle

Rob is running for the US Senate, and this is just the thing those crazy left-wing radical Democrats would like to hang on him? I have been working nonstop to raise over 20 million for his campaign and you can make it disappear in a second."

Sue had never seen her father like this before. Usually he was Mr. Control, and right now she'd hate to take his blood pressure. Trying to reduce the pressure she said, "Dad, you know I would never do anything to hurt Uncle Rob or you. The information I shared with you isn't going anywhere. Delta— that's her name—has no interest in hurting Uncle Rob and doesn't even know if she wants to meet him. She loves her adopted father and is not looking for another one. At the same time, I want you to know that I am an adult and can choose my friends. You are just going to have to accept that."

Her father gave a big sigh and said, "I am going to do a thorough check on this Delta person. First thing tomorrow I will be in contact with my data security company to make sure we haven't been hacked, and I am also calling the head of Executive Protection Services who we hired to provide personal security for the campaign. I am going to get to the bottom of this and will be looking for a big apology when I do. Now what is her full name and where does she live?"

Sue told him that Delta recently changed her last name to Jordan so that it would match her adopted father and prior to that she was Delta Anderson. She also said that Delta was moving back to Greenville where she grew up and she gave him her address. She didn't discuss Delta's telephone number, and figured her father's high and mighty security company could find her. The atmosphere was still cold as ice when they parted.

Delta's phone started ringing and she unconsciously looked at the caller ID and time before answering. It was 8:45 and Sue was calling her. "Hi Sue, what's up?"

Sue responded, "Well, I really did it. I told my father about you and the reality that Uncle Rob is your father."

"Holy shit. Oh, pardon my French. What did he say?"

Sue gave her a verbatim report of their interaction and she didn't leave anything out. Delta became nervous when Sue talked about him contacting the Data Security and the Executive Protection Agency. Anxiety is a strange thing. Delta knew logically there was no reason for her to worry about any investigation into her past or present, but emotionally it had her shaking.

"Well," Delta told Sue, "The cat is out of the bag now and we'll just have to see what happens next. I have to admit if I have a father and half siblings out there, I would like to at least meet them."

Sue said, "You have more relatives than that. You have two first cousins in Todd and me, an uncle and aunt in my parents, and you also have Nana Strong, whom we haven't talked about. She is living in a senior community in Florida and is just a really sweet lady. Grampy Strong died a few years ago."

Delta hadn't thought about all the blood relatives she had, and really didn't know how she felt about them. On one hand, it wasn't like she felt she was missing a part of herself up till this time, but on the other hand she had found how much she liked having a cousin like Sue. Of course that didn't mean the rest of the family would elicit such feelings from her. Nevertheless, going from having no blood relatives to having eight, including Sue's kids, was still mind-blowing.

Chapter 14

Edward Strong tossed and turned in his bed all night long. He kept looking at the alarm clock and the minutes seemed to creep by so slowly. Finally, at 5:30 he couldn't take it any longer and walked to his study to read the online editions of the business and financial papers he subscribed to. By 7:00 he had showered, shaved, and dressed for the day. He pulled the blanket up to cover his wife as she lay sleeping in bed and headed out the door.

He was working at his desk when Angela entered his office with a cup of coffee and a scone. Placing them on the corner of the desk she circled around behind and kissed him on his temple. She said, "Sorry I was late getting out to the lobby to meet your daughter. You don't think she noticed anything, do you?"

Edward said, "She was too preoccupied with other issues to notice you. She was so eager to bring a bunch of crap to me that I now have to deal with. So as soon as you get back to your desk, I want you to get our contact from HTM Data Security on the line. I want to talk to him immediately—and if he isn't available, I want his boss. After that call, I want you to get Jim Smithson from Executive Protection Services on the line. Oh, one last thing—do you know anything about Yourancestor.com?"

Angela had just finished jotting down his first two requests and had to ask him to repeat the third request. Edward went into more detail, "Sue has gotten herself involved with this yourancestor.com and she even had her DNA studied. It sounds like a hokey deal to me and I wanted to know if you were aware of this company."

Angela said, "Of course I have heard of them. They are advertising on TV all the time and I have an aunt that is big into genealogy. I've never heard anything bad about them, other than they charge a pretty hefty monthly fee for their services. There are so many people doing their family trees this day and age that the company has struck gold. If you like, I'll do some more checking on them with the Better Business Bureau and also do some searches on the internet."

Edward's phone rang within a few minutes and Angela announced it was HTM Data Security on the line. After telling his contact person about his concerns, the person said they would keep a close eye on his business but if he wanted something done about his daughter's internet connections, that would cost extra. It turned out that they offered a service to special customers for a fee whereby they would check into a person's computer and literally know everything that was going on. Edward knew they were talking about hacking into her computer, but he didn't think twice about it. He said that he wanted to know everything his daughter was up to. The contact person added that for a complete investigation they could provide him with phone records for any individual. That bit of information sold Edward on the investigation and they quickly agreed on a price. The deal was done.

Within twenty minutes of hanging up with HTM Data Security, he had Jim Smithson on the line. They exchanged the typical pleasantries, and then Edward stated, "Jim, we have a possible problem that needs your attention. My daughter thinks she has made contact with a young woman claiming to be Rob's daughter. I told her she was crazy, but she said the DNA proved it. I need to find out everything you can about one Delta Jordan, AKA Anderson, residing in Greenville, Ohio. She is a recent graduate of U of M. I guess she lives with her adopted father, and her mother is deceased. Pull out all the stops. I want to end all this right now. This girl could really screw up the works for Rob."

Smithson said that he would get right on it and he expected it would be a pretty quick investigation. They arranged to meet in two days. In reality, Edward's biggest worry was for himself, as he had a lot of investors lined up to go with his firm because they wanted Rob's influence in Washington. Edward sat back in his chair and breathed a sigh of relief. He had covered all the bases for now, but was still feeling edgy.

He picked up his phone and pushed the intercom connecting with Angela. "Hey, I'm cutting out in a little while. I really need some special time with you. Can you meet me at 12:00 in our regular room at the Plaza?"

The next day, HTM Data Security had a full report on his desk. His business computers were secure and there had been no attempts at hacking into them. The next several pages were printouts of Sue's computer and cell phone activities. The company had eliminated all the games played by the children and Tom. It did give a list of every site that had been visited. There were no surprises, except for the number of times Sue visited Yourancestry.com. He was hoping that the emails would be proof that Delta was a fraud, but after reading every contact and text she seemed legit. There was nothing in the document file that was of interest. There were copies of letters to relatives and companies along with her financial information. HTM highlighted her financial data and commented that it was not well protected. Of course Edward couldn't do anything about that without letting Sue know that he had hacked into her computer.

It was a couple of days later when Edward met with Jim Smithson, but his report provided no answers. Jim said, "Delta was born in Wood County Ohio to a single 22-year-old mother named Holly Anderson. Holly Anderson lived her entire life in Wood County. She had no work history other than an eighteen-month period of time when she worked for a company called Elite Personal Services. The company provided escort services for men. What may be significant is that the mother was with the escort service at a time that coincides with your brother attending Middle Ohio State. I say this because a contact of mine in the sheriff's office said Elite Personal Services was well known for sending girls to frat houses when they wanted to spice up their parties. The mother stopped working for them before her daughter was born. She also had a lengthy history with the law, including prostitution, and problems with alcohol and drugs. There were also several different incidents involving child protective services, and again most of the charges were because she couldn't care for her child due to her substance abuse.

"There is no record of a father on the birth certificate for Delta Anderson. Through some contacts I learned that Delta was placed in foster care four times and returned to her mother after three of those stays. The last placement was temporary and occurred right after her mother died. The girl started living with a Mr. Oliver Kendall Jordan III, who was reported to be her uncle. He has since legally adopted her. Mr. Jordan is a truck driver who served honorably in the military, including two tours in the Middle East. He has no criminal history and there is virtually no information on him.

"Delta was an honor roll student in school, but there was very little information about her during that time period. I found her listed in the school yearbook, but she was not active in any groups and apparently had few social friends. She worked at Starbucks both in Greenville and in Ann Arbor. She attended U of M and received her BS in chemical engineering. She received some scholarship assistance, but it appears she had money, as there was no loan debt at the time of graduation. It is reasonable to assume Mr. Jordan paid for her college. Oh, also, the home she lives in is jointly deeded to Oliver Jordan and Delta Jordan, formerly Anderson. She has been accepted to four medical schools, which is quite unusual in itself.

"During her years at U of M she kept a low profile. She lived in the same apartment for three years. She had a boyfriend for a couple of years, but there has been no contact since he took a job out of state. She has no criminal record and checking her cell phone activity there is no indication that she is talking with any suspicious people. There is a recent activity that may interest you. Besides her apparent friendship with your daughter, she has established a relationship with your daughter's brother-in-law, a Mr. Brady Blakely. I would assume that your daughter introduced them. The cell phone record shows they talk daily and I would guess they have spent time together. I'm sure you're aware that Brady Blakely is a police officer with the Plymouth Police Department. I think that about covers it. Do you have any questions or want me to look any further?"

Edward could tell his decision wasn't getting any easier. He asked Jim Smithson, as a professional investigator, what he deduced from the investigation. Smithson didn't hesitate, "If I was looking for a smoking gun I would explore the relationship between Elite Personal Services and your brother's fraternity. I did a little checking and your brother belonged to Delta Pi Theta. It is a strange coincidence that Holly would name her daughter Delta. I speculate that Holly was at one of the frat parties and your brother spent time with her. I would also speculate that Holly didn't have a clue as to the name of her child's father. Finally, DNA technology is advancing so rapidly that it is likely the story your daughter told you is true."

"I want this problem to disappear," said Edward. "There is too much at stake for any rumors true or otherwise to surface about Rob. This girl is a major problem to the whole campaign and I need something done about it. We pay you top dollar to provide security, and I expect something back from you."

Smithson replied in a very professional manner. "Executive

Protection Services and I cannot be part of this discussion. I understand what you are asking and we will have no part in it. I am trying to be as clear as possible." As he was talking, Smithson slid a piece of paper over to Edward.

"What is this number?" said Edward as he looked at just a phone number typed on the paper.

"I don't know—it was just lying there. But maybe if you call it they will have some answers for your problem. If you call, don't mention me, and just ask for help with a problem," said Smithson as he left the office.

Edward knew what Smithson was doing. If Smithson was ever called to testify in court he could swear that he told him his company would not be a party to any illegal request. At the same time, Smithson had given him a number to call and basically told him the person on the other end of the line could handle his problem outside the law. He didn't enjoy the thoughts he was entertaining, but knew something major had to be done. He believed he could control his daughter, but didn't think he could prevent this unknown person from talking to the press. The only answer to the problem seemed to be making this newfound daughter of Rob's disappear.

On one hand, Edward would love to rub this problem in Rob's face. His self-righteous brother had actually done something naughty. His younger brother was the chosen child and ever since his birth his parents had been enamored with Rob. Even Edward's success academically and in the financial field paled in their eyes when compared to Rob's success as an evangelist on television. They loved how he was idolized by the thousands and thought he was perfect in all ways. Now Edward had something to throw in Rob's face, and he couldn't do it because too much money rode on Rob being elected.

Edward didn't see any alternative but to call the number Smithson had left him. It rang several times before a man answered. Edward told the person that he had a problem and needed special help with it. The voice on the other end of the line said, "Tomorrow is a great time to visit the aquarium on Belle Isle. I hear the fish are particularly active at two o'clock." He heard a click as soon as the man finished talking. All Edward could think was that this was like some crazy spy story with all these hidden messages. Regardless, he didn't think he had a choice but to visit Belle Isle tomorrow.

Belle Isle is a 982-acre island park in the Detroit River, between the United States and Canada and owned by the City of Detroit. Belle Isle is the largest city-owned island park in the United States and home to the Belle Isle Aquarium along with several other attractions. There is only one bridge going to the island and the aquarium is a major feature that is free to the public. There are usually lots of visitors and no ticket booths or gates to go through. It is perfect place to set up a meeting and at the same time remain inconspicuous.

Edward hadn't been to Belle Isle since his kids were youngsters. The place actually looked in pretty good shape, and that surprised him because he had read about it having hard times over the last decade. There were several cars parked at the aquarium, but it was not crowded by any means. He didn't have any idea how this person would identify him, but figured he might as well enter the building. The beauty of the aquarium built in 1904 amazed him—but then he thought, *No wonder our government is in such bad shape, when we continue to provide this kind of facility free to every Joe Blow?*

He stood looking at one of the fish tanks for minutes, wondering if the mysterious stranger would show up or if he was doing something crazy. A hand tapped him on the shoulder and indicated that Edward should follow him. He led Edward down a short corridor that led to a janitor's closet. He opened the door, turned on the light, and pointed for Edward to step inside. Once in the room the man shut the door and asked Edward to empty his pockets and raise his arms. He checked the items pulled out of the pockets and then started to frisk him.

Edward said, "I'm not carrying a weapon."

The man answered quietly, "I'm not worried about a gun. I want to make sure you are not carrying a wire."

"I would think you'd be more worried about the janitor coming in here."

The man said, "This place is mostly staffed by volunteers and there is absolutely no one here mid-afternoon. Now why don't you tell me what you want and I'll tell you if I can be of assistance."

Edward just started to take notice of the other man. He wasn't an imposing figure in terms of size, but his facial expressions were cold and angry. Edward was unnerved by the man and immediately felt he was someone you don't want to make an enemy of. When Edward started talking, "My name is Edw—" the man interrupted him and said, "I already know your name and where to find you. You will know nothing about me and this will be the only time we will meet. We will not communicate again either in person and only once by phone. So start over and tell me what you want done."

Edward started again, "I have a person that has the potential to cause me great financial harm. I need her to disappear and not be found. I need this to happen within two weeks."

The man answered, "Once I have more information I'll tell you if it can be done within two weeks. I need to know the person's name and where they live."

Edward answered his questions. "Her name is Delta Jordan. She is twenty-two years old and resides in Greenville, Ohio. Her father is a truck driver and on the road most of the time. There is no one else in the house. Here is some background information that Jim Smithson put together on her." Edward handed him a single slip of paper with all the identifying info on it.

The man scanned the paper and then said, "I can make her disappear. It will cost $50,000. I want $25,000 up front and the remainder when the job is complete. I want the money to be in $100 bills. You can leave the money in this room on the top shelf in the box that says hand soap. The box is empty, so there will be plenty of room. I expect it to be here two days from now at this time. Oh, if I don't get the remainder of the money after the job is complete, you won't have to worry about anyone else causing you harm, because you won't be around to know. Do you still want the job done?"

"Yes, but how will I know when the job is done?"

"When she isn't around to cause you harm, you will know the job is done."

Edward left the janitor's closet shortly after the man, and looking around noticed that there weren't any employees and only a few visitors. He would have to get $25,000 ready for the day after tomorrow. He had already thought about how he would handle Sue. Once she couldn't make contact with Delta, he was sure she would come to him. He would steer her in the direction of Delta coming from an unstable background and probably just taking off. He also would say that he didn't think Uncle Rob should be told about the situation until Delta returned. He had always been able to control Sue in the past and didn't think this would be any different.

Back at the office, he told Angela how everything went with the hit man. She was concerned that the man would take the $25,000 and never be heard of again. Edward tried his best to calm her suspicions, but recognized that there were many unknowns with his arrangement. They had formed a unique partnership over the past two years and together had managed to put aside several million dollars by scamming their customers through a Ponzi scheme. It was in both their best interests that Delta be done away with, but if anything went wrong with the plan, they had to be ready to flee the country.

The return trip to the aquarium with the money was uneventful. He had no difficulty placing the money in the janitor's closet, and strangely enough wasn't concerned with it being stolen. Two days later he made the same trip and found the money was no longer in the closet. There was nothing he could do about it now. He did call the phone number that Jim Smithson had given him just to check if the money had been picked up, but the line was out of service. Now he wondered if he was just a sucker who had thrown $25,000 away. Only time would tell.

Chapter 15

I was starting to go stir crazy around Greenville. After four intense years of classes and study it was strange to have free time. Fortunately, Starbucks was very willing to work me a few days a week, which helped a little. I still looked forward to the calls from Brady, but missed seeing him in person. The last time we talked I told him that I was planning to come up for a couple of days over the weekend. In less than eight weeks, I will be heading to Baltimore and starting another four years of schooling. So who knows when I will see Brady again?

Ollie had called me earlier in the day to ask if I could pick him up at the service center where he was having his diesel serviced. The engine had over 500,000 miles on it and there were a number of maintenance issues to be dealt with. I was looking forward to spending a few days with my father alone before I left for school. The last time we were together was graduation, and we really didn't get a chance to talk. I was getting anxious about medical school and knew he had a way of calming me.

He was waiting for me when I arrived at the service center and was as glad to see me as I was to see him. The first part of our trip home was spent talking about his semi. He wanted to get another 500,000 miles out of it and then decide whether to continue driving or retire. We talked about the cost of a new rig, which would set him set back over $100,000 and he didn't know whether it was worth it. I'd never heard him talk about retiring before and I had to wrap my head around the idea. I knew the driving was rough on his back and knees, but still in my mind he was a big strong man.

When we got home we each went our own way. I told him I would prepare dinner and he headed to the basement. When it got close to dinner time I went down in the basement to see what he was up to. I never had a reason to go to the basement and was surprised to find a rather elaborate workshop. He had two work benches, a couple of large electric saws and lots of tools that I had no idea what they did. There were several finished pieces sitting on the floor. What caught my eye was an end table that looked like it was professionally done.

"I can't believe that you built these beautiful woodworking pieces. Have you always had this talent and I didn't know about it?"

Ollie smiled and said, "I always wanted to work with wood, but there was no one to teach me when I was younger. With all the space in the basement I thought it was perfect for a woodshop. I've read lots of magazines and talked a lot to the guys at Home Depot, Lowe's and the local hardware store. Believe me, I have ruined several nice pieces of wood that ended up as scrap. Luckily this old dog has learned some new tricks."

We casually ate our meal while finishing off a bottle of Merlot. Ollie cleaned up after dinner and then we both ended up in the living room. After watching the news and some sitcom reruns, we started talking about the future.

Ollie asked, "Do you think you will be coming home again after you go to medical school? The reason I am asking is this house is half yours and I want to know your opinion about selling."

"You can't sell our house," I moaned. "This is my first real home and it means so much to me. As long as I know that both our home and you are here in Greenville, I will feel safe. I know it's in my head, but it signifies to me that I have a place to go home to. And—don't tell me, because I know I'm being selfish and inconsiderate, so if you really want to sell, I can handle it."

"No, no Delta, I love this house as much as you do. Remember, this is the home that solidified our relationship. This is where we became a real family and I would never want to get rid of it unless that was your desire. If it's okay with you, I want to retire here so you will always have a place to come home to."

I rambled on about my plans after medical school. I talked about becoming a medical researcher particularly focusing on substance abuse and addiction. I have to believe that there was some chemical imbalance in my mother that caused her addiction. I saw her really try to fight it but she always lost the battle. If I could do something to solve that problem, many children would lead better lives.

I said good night, gave him a kiss on the forehead, and went to my room. I soon fell into a sound sleep, but was awakened by someone kneeling on my bed. I screamed out and Ruby started barking just as a hand slapped a piece of duct tape over my mouth. A man dressed in all black had me pinned me to my bed. His knees were on both my arms and he sat on my torso. Even as I was struggling there was enough light in the room for me to see him holding up a syringe.

Just as he was about to inject the contents into me I heard Ollie yell, "What the hell?"

Ollie, with his little dog Ruby right on his heels, came charging into my room. He wrapped the man up in his arms and body slammed him on the floor. They were struggling on the floor when I heard Ollie yell out in pain. He staggered back for an instant, which was just long enough for the man to get up and run. Ollie chased after him, but could only go a few feet before leaning over and grabbing his chest. By the time I turned the light on Ollie was lying on the floor. I ran to him and saw his tee shirt was covered in blood, but the worst part was the knife was still in his chest.

He was losing lots of blood and I was scrambling to save his life. I pulled the tape off my face, grabbed my cell phone, and called 911. As calmly as I could, I told the operator there had been a home invasion and my father had been stabbed. I told her I left the knife in him and would apply a compress to the wound. The last thing I said was "Hurry, because I don't think he is going to make it."

The last time emergency vehicles had been to my house was when my mother died—and Ollie had been part of that too. Now all I could think of was Ollie surviving this attack. I really didn't think I could handle losing Ollie. I ran to the door to make sure it was open for the first responders. The deputy sheriff arrived first and immediately did a check of the whole house. He then took over for me by holding the compress around the wound. Shortly after that, the EMTs rushed through the door and took control of the situation. They were in radio contact with the emergency room and I heard the doctor tell them to leave the knife in the wound until he could be examined at ER. They were giving the vital signs and hooking him up to an EKG and an IV of Ringer's Lactate. They were out the door within a few minutes.

The deputy was very patient with me and knew I wanted to get to the hospital, but he had his job to do too. A man had been stabbed and the assailant was on the run. I gave him all the identifying information such as names, ages and address and phone number. I told him that I was woken from a sound sleep with a man trying to put duct tape on my face. I also told him about the hypodermic needle. I couldn't give much of a description. It was a white male dressed in all black and probably average size, although he had no trouble holding me down on the bed. So I suspected that he was quite strong.

He asked me to stay out of the bedroom while he went in to examine it. In a few minutes he returned and said that he had called the forensic unit so they could complete their part of the investigation. He indicated that the tape and the syringe were still in the room. I told him I had to get to the hospital, but couldn't go in my pajamas. He questioned whether I was okay to make the drive and then allowed me to get clothes and shoes from the closet.

The deputy said that he had to stay at the house till the

forensic unit arrived and he would make sure the house was secure before he left. I learned that a detective would be assigned to the case and more than likely would want to talk to me right away. So I was not surprised when my cell phone rang and it was Detective George Miller. He explained that the deputy had given him my number and he emphasized the importance of interviewing me right away. I agreed to meet him at the hospital.

I was directed to the surgical waiting room and told that my father was in surgery and that the surgeon would talk to me after surgery was complete. It was now after 1:30 and I was feeling so alone. The first person I thought about calling was Brady. I held off for about twenty minutes and then couldn't stop myself from calling him. I could tell that I woke him up but was so relieved to hear his voice.

"Brady, this is Delta."

"Delta, what's wrong? Your voice is trembling."

"It's my father—an intruder stabbed him and I don't know if he is going to live. He was just trying to protect me as he always does, and the man stabbed him and ran."

He tried to ask questions but I just was all over the place. I think I got out most of the information out, but who knows if I made sense. The phone call came to an abrupt end when a man came into the waiting room and asked if I was Delta Jordan.

The man, who introduced himself as Detective George Miller, looked to be in his fifties, with grey hair, ruddy complexion, and a slight belly hanging over his belt. With a note pad and pen in hand he asked if we could take a seat and talk. He started slowly and repeated himself often. I don't know if that was to be clear on the answer or if my answers weren't making sense. It was like a lot of the reruns of *Columbo* that Ollie and I watched on occasion.

"Miss Jordan, when did you know there was an intruder in your house?"

"We both went to bed a little after eleven and the first time I looked at a clock after the attack it was almost twelve. I was rather busy trying to keep my father alive and didn't think about the time."

The detective talked in a quiet but firm style. "So he entered your house sometime between 11:15 and 11:40. Your call to 911 was at 11:45 and the deputy reported arriving at your house at 11:55, which is when you probably had time to look at a clock. With these next questions please take your time and try to remember everything including what you were thinking at the time. Walk me through everything that happened from the time you woke up till the time the intruder ran from the house."

I took a few seconds to gather my thoughts and then answered, "The first thing I remember is my bed sinking on one side kind of like someone was sitting on it. Immediately this man swung his leg over my body and straddled me. He had his legs and knees positioned in such a way that my arms were pinned to the mattress and I couldn't squirm from under him. I was thinking that I was going to be raped. When I saw the tape coming toward my mouth I managed to scream once or twice. Then he had my mouth covered with tape and I couldn't scream. My next thought was that I would suffocate, which caused me to start hyperventilating.

"I can tell you the man was dressed in black with a black ski mask over his face. He had some kind of gloves on that looked like a doctor would use. I couldn't figure out why he had the syringe in his hand and even thought that was strange if he was going to rape me. He never tried taking my clothes off or groping me. The next thing I remember is hearing my father yell something and Ruby barking like crazy. My father is huge and he hit the man with a lot of force. They both went tumbling off the bed and I heard thumps and bangs, but couldn't see anything. Oh—my father yelled out like he was hurt, and the man ran with my father trying to grab him. He only ran a few feet before he dropped. Luckily the intruder didn't know how bad my father was injured, or he might have come back for me."

"Is there anyone who is angry at you and may want to hurt you? You know, like former boyfriends or someone at work... just anybody at all."

His question shook me up because it never occurred to me that someone could be trying to hurt me. "No, I don't have anybody angry at me. My last boyfriend left the state over a year ago and we broke up on good terms. I've been too busy with school and work to be socially active, but I honestly can't think of anyone who would want to hurt me. In all reality, I am the type of person that many people would call a wallflower. I have never tried to attract attention and usually manage to keep off people's radar."

Detective Miller stayed around asking questions for the next hour. Mostly, they were the same questions phrased a different way in hopes that it would elicit a new memory or thought on my part. Before he left he gave me his card and said, "We want to get on this right away. If you think of anything else, call me at this number day or night. The forensic unit has finished by now and I just want to prepare you that they don't leave things neat. They dusted for fingerprints and found where he probably forced the lock on the front door. Your house is so secluded; he probably had no fear breaking in the front door. I have to tell you that the syringe is not common in a rape case, which is why I questioned about someone being angry at you. I also couldn't believe a person would enter your house with a man as big as your father in the same place."

His statement brought something to mind. "Detective, I don't think the man knew my father was home, and if that is true it means he was really after me. My father drives a semi-tractor and if he is home the truck is in the drive. This week he is having work done on it and I picked him up at the repair shop. So anyone watching our home who knows us would assume that I am alone."

As the detective was getting ready to leave, Brady came rushing through the door. The first thing he did was take me in his arms and for the first time in hours I felt safe. When I looked at the detective, I could tell he was interested. He immediately said, "I thought you said there were no boyfriends in the picture?"

"Excuse me, Detective; let me introduce you to Brady Blakely. Brady, this is Detective George Miller with the Wood County Sheriff's Department. Brady is my cousin's brother-in-law, and more recently, a friend of mine."

Brady immediately stepped forward with his outreached hand. "Detective, As Delta said I am Brady Blakely. I am also on the job as a patrol officer with the Plymouth, Michigan police department. Delta called me a little over an hour ago and I came down immediately. Do you mind if we talk outside for a minute?"

And with that request, the two of them walked off like old buddies. If I hadn't been so tired and worried about Ollie, I probably would have been furious to be cut out of the conversation. In about ten minutes, Brady returned and sat next to me. He put his arm on my shoulder and said, "I didn't want you to think I was doing a macho thing with the detective, but I thought he may say some things to me he wouldn't share with you. He was more interested in our relationship than I thought he would be. He said that one didn't have to be a detective to see there was more going on between us than just friends. I told him that we had only been on a couple of dates but I wanted the relationship to be more than friends."

His words made me uncomfortable, because I was trying to keep the boyfriend thing under control. I didn't want to start medical school 700 miles away and be hurting over leaving my boyfriend. At the same time, he was acting just like I would expect an attentive boyfriend to act. He rushed to my side to comfort me and then tried to find some answers from the detective.

Brady didn't tell me anything I didn't know. Detective Miller thought that I was the target. He also didn't think it was going to be a rape. The crime lab had the syringe, tape, bed linens, and my night wear and they would be looking for DNA evidence. He also told Brady that since I live in a rural area they probably wouldn't get any help from neighbors. Nevertheless, the sheriff's department would go door to door tomorrow asking questions.

It was about 4:30 when a doctor entered the waiting room, still in his surgical gown. The doctor approached me, introduced himself and asked if I was with Oliver Jordan. I told him I was his daughter and wanted to know how he was doing. The doctor suggested we sit down, and then proceeded to give a detailed report.

"He is stable at this time and in ICU, but it was a difficult surgery. He had some good things in his favor. The knife was a slender switch blade, so the entry into the chest didn't do much damage. Also, leaving the knife in the chest was a good decision, because any wrong move pulling it out of his chest could have cut the aorta. The bottom line is that he is stable, his vitals look good, and he will probably make a full recovery. You can see him for about ten minutes every hour until he is moved to a regular room. He's not awake at this time, but should be waking up in a few hours."

I asked if they kept the knife and the doctor chuckled. "We may not have many knife wounds with the knife still in the victim, but we do know police protocol. The knife has been preserved and will be picked up by the sheriff." Before he left he told me where the ICU was located and said that he would be checking on my father in the morning.

Brady walked with me to the ICU and we talked with a nurse at the desk. She said the same thing as the doctor—that I would be able to see him for ten minutes each hour. Brady said that he would wait in the waiting area. My mind was getting clearer and I thought about something he could do to really help me.

"Brady, can I ask you a big favor? It would be a huge help if you would go to my house and make sure my dad's dog, Ruby is okay. There is food in the bottom cupboard by his dishes and a leash hanging by the door. She needs fresh water, food, and a walk. Would you mind doing that so I can stay here?"

Brady was more than willing to go to my home. I had to give him directions although he said his GPS could direct him. I gave him the key and then asked if he would mind getting a change of clothes for me. I was very specific about what drawers to go into and just wanted jeans, a top, panties, and socks. I wrote down a list of the items so there shouldn't be a question.

After getting my keys, he pulled me close and said, "I'm here for you and will do anything to make this easier." A quick kiss on the lips and he was out the door.

My first visit with Dad was terrible. He looked so grey and with all the IVs inserted in his arm and the monitors that kept beeping, I was scared. He didn't move, so I sat there and held his hand. All I could do was to tell him he was going to be okay and that I loved him. I said it over and over. The nurse came in to check on him and tell me that my time was up. She wasn't really friendly, but did share that everything was going as expected. I guess it was more important that she was skilled rather than friendly.

My next visit with Ollie went better, and I thought he looked more like himself. I know part of my struggle was seeing this big, strong man that I put on a pedestal look weak and old. Ollie was the one always making sure I was okay and this role reversal wasn't something I liked. As I sat holding his hand, I noticed his breathing seemed more comfortable, and his color was definitely better.

Brady arrived back at the hospital before the third visit. He had found a carry-on bag and packed it with the needed items, plus other things such as toothbrush and toothpaste. I noticed he also threw extra bra and underwear in the bag, so he must have been through every drawer.

He looked sheepish and said, "I also found this other electronic device, but didn't think you'd need it here."

At this point I was too tired to be embarrassed and said, "OH, you must have found BOB?"

"BOB?" he questioned.

"Yes, BOB, my battery-operated boyfriend." For the first time in hours I chuckled and as soon as I said it I knew our relationship had moved to a whole new level.

Brady started laughing and grabbed me in his arms and

said, "You're too much. Oh, by the way I have Ruby out in my car. I didn't know how long you were going to stay here and thought it was easier to bring her with me. Don't worry—I found her food and water bowls so she is comfy in the car. Before you can say it, the windows are cracked open too."

I ended up staying at the hospital through that day and night. I didn't feel comfortable even thinking about leaving till I knew Ollie was going to make it. When he opened his eyes and looked at me I just burst into tears. I had never been so scared of losing someone in my life.

Chapter 16

I was so glad to be home, and nothing felt better than when I collapsed on my own bed. Brady had stayed with me as long as he could, but had to get back to work. Taking care of Ruby at the hospital wasn't bad, because it gave me something to do to keep my mind off of my father. However, even Ruby seemed to be overjoyed being home and ran around like a pup. The doctor said Ollie might be able to come home in three days. He wanted to be sure there was no internal bleeding and that everything was healing correctly.

My phone rang, waking me from my unplanned nap shortly before 5:00 p.m. It was Detective Miller and he told me that the results were back from the lab on the material inside the syringe. He asked if I would be home, because he was fifteen minutes away and wanted to talk to me in person. I could tell by the sound of his voice that he was serious.

When he got to my home he started talking immediately while reading from a piece of paper in his hand. "Ms. Jordan, the laboratory report says that the contents of the syringe were a mixture of hydroxyacetic acid, butoxyethanol, monohexyl ether, alcohol, bleaches and enzymes."

When I asked what they are used for he responded, "I asked the very same question and found out that it is a pretty common substance. Once you get rid of the scientific names, what you have is the ingredients in a commercial rug cleaning solution you can buy at any hardware store. However, more important to know is that the lab told me that death is a sure thing if it got injected into you."

I was stunned and couldn't think of anything to say. After a little silence Detective Miller continued, "It is pretty clear that this was an attempt on your life and not a rape or kidnapping. The fact that the solution was identifiable leads me to believe that he wasn't intending for anyone to find you or think your death was an accident. I think he planned to kill you in your bed and then get rid of your body in another location. You have to realize that this is a very unusual situation. I did a thorough records check on both you and your father and couldn't find anything to explain this murder attempt. Somebody has it out for you, and you are still at risk. I am not comfortable with you staying here alone and our department doesn't have the resources to assign an officer for your security. Do you have any place you can go, at least until your father gets home from the hospital?"

I was kind of embarrassed to say that I didn't have any place to go. The only possibility was Sue's house and that would be really bold of me to ask if I could stay there. The detective was relentless and I finally said I would call my cousin. Sue answered on the second ring and sounded really upbeat.

"What's up, cuz?"

"Sue, have you talked with Brady?"

"No, we just got back from a couple of days at a friend's cottage on Drummond Island and the cell reception was terrible. Why, do you need to talk with him?" she asked.

I took a deep breath and started talking nonstop. "Sue, someone broke in my house the other night and tried to kill me. I was lucky my father was home and the person obviously didn't know he was here, because his truck wasn't at the house as it was being serviced. He fought the guy but ended up being stabbed in the chest. The hospital performed emergency surgery and thankfully it looks as if he is going to make it."

Sue couldn't believe what i was telling her. She wasn't surprised when I told her that Brady drove down to Greenville and stayed with me at the hospital the first day. Sue told me that Brady really had feelings for me, so it didn't surprise her. I also told her about the duct tape and syringe. She was particularly alarmed when I told her about the caustic solution. Trying to be light-hearted I said that I didn't know what I had done to tick someone off, but I must have really done it good.

Before I could ask about coming to her house, she said, "Pack your bag right this minute and get up here. No way are you staying there alone. If you don't get up here tonight I will send Tom down to get you."

All I could say was "Do you know Ruby has to come with me?" and "Thank you."

Detective Miller stayed at the house until I was packed and watched me drive away. I don't know if I was paranoid or not, but there seemed to be a car following me as soon as I pulled out of the driveway. I didn't see the car once I was on the expressway, and pretty soon I zoned out and didn't pay attention to much of anything the rest of the drive. As soon as I arrived at Sue's house, she came running out the door and threw her arms around me. I just started sobbing uncontrollably and Sue held me as tight as she could. We didn't enter the house till all my tears were dry and I was more under control. Meanwhile, Ruby was going bonkers in my car.

Peter and Alison ran down the stairs to greet me and their hugs made all my worries lighten. "Aunt Delta, you're going to be staying in the room next to mine. Come on, I'll show you," said Peter as he pulled me up the stairs. Then they saw Ruby and I was yesterday's news. All they wanted to do was play with the pup. Sue was trying her best to call the kids off, but I told her to relax. After showing me the guest room, both Peter and Alison had to give me a tour of their bedrooms. They were equally excited about having me there and trying to impress me with things in their room, but it was Ruby who they were really interested in.

Once the kids were settled for the night Sue, Tom, and I sat in the living room. Sue and I were sipping wine, but Tom said this situation called for a beer. Finally, the three of us with drinks in hand were ready to talk. I told them everything that had happened to me from the time I picked up my father at the service center to the time Detective Miller watched me drive away tonight. I even told them about the car I thought was following me and then joked about being paranoid. Tom tried to humor me with the old standby, "Just because you're paranoid doesn't mean they're not out to get you." I laughed at first, but then thought, *What if it's the truth?*

Sue said that she hadn't heard back from her father since she told him about me and his silence bothered her. It was her thought that he should have discussed it with Uncle Rob by now. I tried to assure her that I didn't want to put pressure on anyone in her family, particularly Rev. Rob. In fact, I was really happy just knowing I had cousins in Sue, Peter, and Alison. Sue wouldn't let it drop and said that she was going to pay her father a visit tomorrow. Sue said that he was too good at dismissing her when they were on the phone. After a few drinks everyone was mellow and we headed off to bed.

I slept very soundly in Sue's guest room, but was woken up by the sound of glass breaking and a woman's scream. I checked my cell phone and saw that it was 7:47 in the morning. I guess I really had a great sleep, but then I thought about the sound that woke me up. I listened and couldn't hear any other noise. Slowly I climbed out of bed, slipped into some jeans, and headed down stairs. When I entered the kitchen I found Sue sitting on the floor with her back to a cupboard. Blood was running down her forehead and she looked dazed. As I was running to her side I noticed the window over the sink had been shattered. I grabbed a dish towel and knelt next to Sue.

When I made eye contact with Sue she said, "I think I've been shot?"

She told me that she was in the kitchen making coffee after Tom had headed off to work. The kids were still in bed so she thought she would get "a little me time." When she went to the sink to refill the coffee pot she heard a pop sound and felt something hit her head. I slowly got up and peeked out the window. The view from the kitchen window was of the back yard and the perimeter of the yard was rimmed with full grown cedar trees. I couldn't see anybody around, but somebody must have figured out that I was at Sue's house.

Sue was trying to stand up, but I told her to remain seated. I gave her the towel and went to the phone to dial 911. At first Sue was trying to dissuade me and said she didn't want to upset the kids. I wasn't going to accept her reasoning and dialed 911 anyway. I told the operator that a shot had been fired into a home in Northville and someone was injured. Sue gave me the address and other information that the officer needed. After hanging up I asked Sue for Tom's cell phone number and made a call to him. Tom had a little difficulty comprehending that his wife had possibly been shot. He said he was turning around and would be home in just minutes. Then together Sue and I waited sitting on the kitchen floor till we heard the sirens.

Within minutes, we were swamped with emergency personnel, including a fire truck, which apparently is sent out on every call in her town. They confirmed that Sue had been shot at and we saw where the bullet had penetrated the kitchen wall. Fortunately, the bullet missed her, but some flying glass hit her head. Although the only medical treatment she needed was a small bandage, they told her she would have to go to the hospital because it was a firearm incident. The police officer took detailed notes about the situation, including the previous assault on my life. After calling into the station he informed me that he would be staying with me until a detective from the Northville PD. arrived. Tom came running through the door shortly thereafter and immediately went to comfort Sue. After some discussion, Tom said he would accompany Sue to the hospital if I would look out for the children.

Northville must have more resources then Greenville, because they didn't think twice about assigning an officer to stay with me. Since we couldn't touch anything in the kitchen till forensics had done their thing, I grabbed some cereal, milk, bowls, spoons, and bananas to feed the children. I was surprised they slept through most of the noise, but by 8:25 both Peter and Alison were awake and downstairs. They were full of questions, but since they didn't see their bloody mother, they didn't get upset. I was able to keep them in the TV room. I told them their mother had a little cut and was seeing a doctor but would be home shortly. In the meantime, they thought that eating cereal in the TV room was a great treat.

The detective arrived just before Sue and Tom got home. I didn't want to talk in front of the children and he was patience enough to wait for their return. When Sue and Tom got home, the kids had all sorts of questions, but seeing that Sue only had a small bandage on her head helped them accept her rendition of the events. Tom took the kids to the park so that we could talk with the detective. I was awash with guilt as I shared what had happened to me in Greenville. I told them that I probably was the reason for Sue's injury and I had to get away from them so they wouldn't be hurt.

It was weird that all these things were happening to me and I couldn't explain why. Sue had been shot at because of me, and as I thought more about it I realized that we look so much alike the shooter could have mistaken us. Sue had already been thinking the same thing. So here I am with two people I really care about, my father and Sue, nearly killed because of me, and yet I didn't have an answer. I did check in with my father while Sue was at the hospital so he wouldn't worry if he tried to contact me, but I didn't talk about the incidents today.

The police decided that it was best if I stayed with the Blakely's for the time being and assigned am officer to watch over us. Sue and Tom didn't question it for a minute and said in no way would they let me leave. By dinner time we were all hungry and ordered out for pizza to feed the crowd that had gathered at the house. Sue's parents, Edward and Ann, arrived in the late afternoon. Tom's parents and Brady came over around supper time, so the house was full of relatives. The Strong's immediately took Sue aside and were trying to comfort her. Her father seemed really upset about Sue's injury and I even heard him question why she let me stay in the house. Brady grabbed my hand and pulled me into another room, and the Blakely's took Peter and Alison out to the yard to play.

This was a heck of a way to meet my biological uncle and his wife, as well as my potential future boyfriend's parents. Brady's parents were warm and comforting. I could tell by the way they treated the grandchildren that they were caring people. Sue's parents, on the other hand, were much more restrained and aloof. I knew they were worried about Sue, but they kept a distance. Hearing her father's demand that she should stay away from me was very disconcerting. Sue had warned me about them, so I was prepared when I saw their difficulty comforting her. In many ways my mother was a lot like Sue's mother. Emotions were not displayed openly by my mother, so I was not surprised by Sue's parents.

Brady was more concerned about me than ever. Two attempts on my life were really making him jumpy. While we were outside he held me and constantly kissed my forehead, telling me he was going to protect me. The only thought going through my head was *Protect me from what?* I didn't have the slightest clue who wanted to do me harm, but I knew without a doubt that anyone close to me could be hurt.

While we were having pizza, Sue introduced me to everyone. She shared information about our relationship and announced that I was her newfound cousin. I was watching the reactions of the people and saw that Edward was very disturbed. His wife Ann seemed to be confused, and of course Tom's parents didn't have a clue what she was talking about. Sue explained the whole sequence of events, starting with the first DNA test from yourancestor.com. The Blakely's were enthralled with the story and kept talking about it being amazing. Ann Strong seemed stunned by her daughter's story, but the really interesting reaction was from Edward. He tried to interrupt and redirect Sue from the minute she started talking. He kept saying nothing has been proved yet and we shouldn't rush to judgment.

What I did notice is that most everyone there accepted me as belonging, whether I was family or not. Once Sue's mother got over her apparent confusion, she talked about how much Sue and I looked alike. She didn't broach the issue of Rev. Rob being my father, but it was clear that she thought there was some family connection. Edward never talked directly with me the whole evening. After dinner the kids were sent to watch TV and Sue gave the family a complete report of the attempts on her and my life. She didn't hold back any information, including the attack on me, my father's stabbing, and the possibility that she was shot because she looked like me. She ended by saying it was clear that someone was trying to kill me, and she almost lost her life because of it.

Edward took the floor and while looking at me said in angry voice, "I am not going to stand by and see my daughter injured because of this person that we have basically just met." Looking at me, he said, "You never should have come here and I want you to leave and never come back. You come to this family with all your concocted stories and think we will accept you as family—well, you are sadly mistaken." You could hear the gasps in the room. I tried to talk but couldn't form a sentence. Sue was the first to speak and she said, "Dad, that is enough. Whether you want to believe it or not, Delta is my cousin and I love her. If staying in our house keeps her safe, then I want her to stay here and I think it would be a good idea if you left right now."

Edward turned to Ann, his wife, and said, "I can tell when I'm not wanted. Ann, get your things—we are leaving." He was out the door before anyone could say another word. The rest of the family was bewildered by Edward's tirade and subsequent actions. Sue turned to me and said, "I am truly sorry for my father's behavior and I do not agree with him one bit." She then turned to Tom's parents and apologized again for her father's behavior. They tried to excuse it by saying that he was just too worried about her, but it sounded unconvincing even as they said it. The gathering broke up quickly, with the Blakely's heading home. Brady stayed around a while longer to try to comfort me, but eventually had to get home.

Sue, Tom, and I stayed up talking for a while longer, but eventually we headed up to bed. Knowing the police were outside should have been comforting, but it didn't help me at all. Sleep didn't come easy like the night before, and by the next morning I felt I hadn't slept at all. This whole episode was like a nightmare that I couldn't wake up from. The more I thought about it, the more confused I became.

Chapter 17

Sue and Tom were in the kitchen when Delta came down for breakfast. She could hear the TV in the family room and assumed the kids were already down too. Sue had coffee ready for Delta and played the good hostess by asking what she would like for breakfast. At that point Delta had zero appetite, but told Sue just toast, to be accommodating. After asking her how she was feeling, Sue said, "Oh, the head wound is just fine, but I'm not fine otherwise. I am going to talk to my father again. His behavior last night was bizarre and inexcusable."

Delta tried to talk her out of it, but to no avail. Sue asked Delta if she would look after the kids this morning while she visited her father, because Tom would be at work. Delta knew she couldn't refuse her after all she has done for her including risking her own life?

Sue stomped into her father's office by passing the foyer. Angela was sitting at the reception area inside the office and immediately got up when Sue entered. She asked Sue if she could be of help and Sue said she needed to talk with her father. When Angela told her that he was out of the office till 10:00, Sue said, "That's okay, I'll wait," and walked past her into his office. She had never done anything like this before, and for some reason didn't even worry whether her father would blow his stack.

Once in his office alone, she started to have different

thoughts and almost talked herself out of staying there. At first she sat down across from his desk and then got antsy and walked around. Eventually she ended up behind his desk and started looking at the stacks of papers on each corner. Sue started to feel weird and guilty looking at her father's personal stuff on his desk, but then something caught her eye. It was her cell phone number circled in red. There in front of her was a cell phone report that not only had her number but it identified every incoming and outgoing call she had made, and the names of the people involved in the call. She picked up the paper to be sure she wasn't mistaken and saw that he had detailed information for the past several months.

Sue was livid. She was an adult that had been on her own for years. There was no reason for her father to have her cell phone information, and yet there it was. She felt violated and couldn't do a thing about it. As she was stewing about the information her father walked into the office. At first he tried to be high-handed and act indignant by scolding her, "What are you doing looking at papers on my desk?"

Sue wasn't shaken at all by his angry outburst and calmly said, "Oh Daddy, what have you done?"

For the first time in her life she saw her father as a fallible man. It was as if he shrank within seconds and was no longer the powerful wheeler-dealer. Edward collapsed in his chair and said, "I did what I thought would be best for the whole family and I don't know how to stop it." Before he could even start telling her what had happen he burst into an angry retort. "I had so much riding on Rob's election that I lost myself in the process. I don't know if you'll ever forgive me for putting your life at risk. I thought that I had it all under control."

"What have you done, Daddy?"

Edward seemed to be regaining some of his old condescending attitude. He told Sue about everything, including hiring a hit man. All the time he kept trying to convince her that he was doing it for their family and Uncle Rob. He tried to justify his actions by saying he only wanted Delta to disappear and never really thought about her being killed. What really shocked her was that he sarcastically said, "I must have hired the most incompetent hit man around." Sue never in her wildest imagination could have predicted what was transpiring with her father. She knew he wasn't a warm and toasty father like some of her friends' fathers, but at the same time she always thought he was in their corner.

Sue was so flustered she didn't know whether to run, call the police, or call Uncle Rob, so she said, "You've got to stop this man. I can't believe you would hire a killer. I always knew you were cold to me and withholding of affection, but I never thought even you would go this far." The last question she asked was, "Does Uncle Rob know about this?"

His answer was brief: "No." Edward looked beaten. "I can't stop him. His contact number which was given to me is now no longer in service. I called the person that gave me the number and he acted as if he didn't know what I was talking about. At the time he said he would never do anything to break the law but then handed me the paper with a phone number on it. There is no way I can prove that he led me to that person.

This is going to ruin me. I needed some major new investors to cover some bad decisions I made, and if Rob isn't elected senator they won't invest a penny with me."

That statement was the straw that broke the camel's back. Sue ran from her father's office before he had a chance to say anything else. As soon as she was out the door he called Angela into the office. Angela had been more than his assistant for the last few years. She was his lover, co-conspirator and confidant. When she entered the office he said, "Everything is falling apart rapidly and we need to go to Plan B."

Plan B was their emergency plan that would allow them to escape any kind of prosecution—and with lots of money, too. When he first shared with Angela the information about Rob fathering an illegitimate child, she didn't have any suggestions as to what they should do. Their plan was always to get an influx of new money so they could keep paying high returns to some of their customers and they were relying on Rev. Rob to attract the customers. All the while they had secreted millions of dollars of their customers' money into an offshore account. When Edward suggested hiring a hit man to kill this girl, Angela didn't balk at all.

They spent months looking for the safest place to put their money and also where they could run to themselves if everything caved in. Angela was the one who found the best place for them. By studying online and talking with other knowledgeable money people she identified Andorra as the place for them. This tiny low-tax nation nestled high in the mountains between France and Spain has long been a favorite of wealthy Europeans. Today, despite all the turmoil in the rest of Europe, Andorra has one of the best capitalized banking systems on the continent. Lots of Americans had money in the banks there too, and best of all, Andorra did not have an extradition agreement with the US.

It just so happened that Angela's extended family was from Spain and she spoke Spanish fluently. Although the official language of Andorra was Catalan, most of the people also spoke Spanish. Edward took Spanish in college, but to improve his communication skills he bought the Rosetta Stone Language program. Two years ago Edward told his wife Ann that he was going to an international financial conference in Madrid. At that time, Ann had already given up on Edward and their marriage. She didn't even ask where it was being held or when he was getting back. Edward and Angela registered for the conference and then flew on to Andorra where they opened accounts in banks that could handle their money transfers.

Edward was pissed that the hit man screwed up, but he didn't feel any guilt over the attempted murder. He had worked too hard to lose it now because his damn brother wasn't smart enough to use a condom twenty-three years ago. He didn't feel obligated to the idiots that invested with him, and saw them as whiners and babies. If market dropped a bit, they would be on the phone crying about their loses even when he reminded them they hadn't lost anything till they sold. When they got a 10% return they talked about a friend that got 14%. They were just rich SOBs who didn't deserve the money they had, and thus he justified his theft of it.

When Sue got to her uncle's house, Aunt Michele answered the door and was surprised to see her standing there. Aunt Michele's first response after seeing the bandage on her head was to ask her if she was okay. Sue had no time for small talk and said that she needed to see Uncle Rob right now. Michele tried to get her to relax and again asked if there was anything she could do. When that failed, she said that she would get him.

Rob had been alerted to Sue's apparent distress by his wife and entered the foyer saying, "What's the matter, Susie?"

He wrapped his arms around her in an embrace and for a brief moment Sue felt as if things were going to be all right. Uncle Rob was always the father figure that knew how to give her reassurance and take away her hurts. Then everything that had happened came crashing down on her and she knew things wouldn't be all right ever again once she told Uncle Rob the whole story. She knew her family would never be the same again, and this terrified her. She thought it would be best if she could speak to him in private, and he led her back to his study.

Sue didn't know where to start, so she just rambled. "I've kept something from you, something that I have known about for several months. I kept it from you because I didn't know what to do and went to my father for help. What he did is terrible and I don't know how I am going to fix the situation." Sue was sobbing at this point and Uncle Rob, not knowing the severity of the problem, hugged her and said everything will be all right. All she could do was to shake her head and say, "No, it won't—no."

Rob's calm eventually won out and Sue began telling him everything, starting with the DNA test. "Uncle Rob, I think you remember that I was doing our family tree a couple of years ago. When Tom learned so I was so interested in genealogy he bought me a DNA test through yourancestor.com. That DNA test uncovered something that I never expected and the information has changed my life and most certainly will change yours." He didn't interrupt and let her continue.

"The results showed that my DNA matched another person and classified this person as my 1st cousin. I met this cousin, whose name is Delta several months ago, and at first was skeptical about the relationship but quickly we both came to the realization that she was my cousin. Furthermore, the only person that could have fathered her was you."

At this point Uncle Rob became animated and irritated, "Hold up, Sue—I have never cheated on my wife and never fathered a child. This is just crazy talk and probably something my political enemies created. Has this girl asked you for money yet?"

"It's not like that, Uncle Rob. Delta graduated from U of M in chemical engineering. She is twenty-two years old and lives in Greenville, Ohio. I contacted her, she didn't contact me. Delta has been accepted to every medical school she applied to. She was not looking to cash in on something and if anything, we have messed up her life. Delta and I have spent lots of time together and I can honestly say I love her. I am convinced you are her biological father and I am also convinced that you didn't know about her. There is so much more I have to tell you, but first let me show you these."

Sue turned on her cell phone and showed her uncle several pictures of Delta. His first response was to say, "My God, she looks so much like Melissa they could be twins. This has to be a scam. I don't remember any relationship that could have led to a baby being born." He was trying to convince himself at the same time he stared at the pictures. Rob went back to his seat and just about collapsed in it.

Sue continued, "Uncle Rob, the reason I came over here in such a panic is that something horrible is happening to Delta and if I don't do something, her life is in danger. I went to my father with the information about Delta a month ago. He didn't believe it and hired an investigator to check her out. Apparently the investigator convinced him that she is your daughter, because of information he learned about the mother. That was all it took for my father to hire someone to kill her. He thought any word of an illegitimate child would derail your campaign." Rob was flabbergasted and couldn't put any words together to make a sentence.

Sue struggled on. "The killer made an attempt on Delta's life a few days ago and was unsuccessful. He did, however, stab her adoptive father in the process and nearly killed him. Her father is still in the hospital in Greenville. The police didn't want Delta to stay in her home alone and I told her to come to my house. Yesterday morning while I was in the kitchen I was hit by a gunshot through my kitchen window. Thankfully it just grazed me, but the bottom line is the police think it was another attempt on Delta's life. The police had completed a thorough investigation on Delta and her father and could find no reason why someone would want to harm her. They didn't know that my father had hired a killer to eliminate her. I just found out myself this morning."

Sue started to become concerned about her uncle. He was rocking back and forth and saying over and over, "Oh my lord." She realized that he was having difficulty making sense of what she was saying. He kept asking, "What was Edward thinking? Why would he try to take someone's life? Didn't he trust me enough to come to me with the information? I could have told him it wasn't possible."

Sue started again. "That's just the point I am trying to make, Uncle Rob. It is possible. The DNA information is very accurate—and on top of that the investigator that my father hired learned that Delta's mother worked for an escort service that worked the fraternity parties at Middle Ohio U. On top of that she often worked for your fraternity the same time that you were there. Delta's mother died when Delta was fifteen but she always kidded her that she had gotten her name from a fraternity because that was where she was made."

Her uncle became extremely quiet and for the first time since she started this discussion he didn't seem to be forming arguments in his mind as she spoke. It seemed as if he had remembered something, and with regaining this memory pieces were beginning to fall into place. Finally, he said, "Sue, I will need all the documentation that you have and also I am asking you to be quiet about this until I have had a chance to think about it and talk with your Aunt Michele and the kids.

"I also have to be very direct with you—and it hurts me because he is your father and I know you love him. Your father has made lots of decisions in his life that were based on what's good for him. I really don't think he was trying to help me by arranging a murder. Once again, he was looking out for himself. Throughout my life he has criticized the way I led my life and made fun of the moral values that I preached about. I'm sorry to say it, but your father has many flaws in his character and I am afraid that he made a really bad decision with the information you gave him. So I need to talk with your father right away and try to figure out what was going through his mind. You should know that based on that discussion I will be calling the police to report what you told me. Equally important, where is Delta now and when can I meet her?"

Sue answered, "The last time I talked with her she was at my home watching the kids. There is a police officer on duty there, but you have to realize her life is in danger and my father cannot stop the man from attempting to kill her again."

Sue dialed the number expecting to reach Delta, and Tom answered the phone.

Chapter 18

I was surprised when Tom came through the kitchen door. He told me that he was useless at work after what happened yesterday. His first reaction was to look for the kids and he was pleased to see them sitting at the kitchen table drawing pictures. Although they both yelled his name when they saw him, they remained glued to their seats. I explained that they were drawing a picture that I could take back to my house. I told them that I didn't have children and missed them when I was at home. A picture drawn by them would be a wonderful reminder.

Peter said, "Aunt Delta, you are going to love this picture when I am done."

I stayed at Sue and Tom's house till mid-afternoon but I started feeling guilty about not seeing my father. I knew the police wouldn't let me go alone, but Brady came in to save the day. Brady's first shift ended at 2:30 and he caught me off guard when he pulled into the driveway at 3:00. I talked to him about my need to visit my father and he took it from there. I saw Brady talking with the supervising officer outside and I burst into a big grin when he gave me the thumbs-up sign.

The drive down was rather cathartic. It took over an hour and a half so we had a chance to unwind. Our conversation was very much like the way we talked on the phone at night. He was supportive, but not too pressuring. Neither of us knew much about the outcome of Sue's conversation with her dad or Rev. Rob. She had texted us that she told Rev. Rob and he was shocked, but he also was asking for time to think through the situation. I texted her that Brady and I were going to my house in Greenville and Rev. Rob could have all the time he needed.

When I reached my father's hospital room, things were really looking up. Ollie's color was getting better and better and all the tubes were removed except for one IV, which was supposed to be removed in a few hours. If all went well, he would be released tomorrow. I didn't want to upset him so I started out gently. I told him that Ruby was out in the car and that the service center had called and his truck was ready to be picked up. After lots of small talk I decided that he should know about Sue being hit by a bullet yesterday. He asked many questions, to which I had very few answers. When it was apparent that Ollie was becoming overly concerned, Brady told him he was taking the next few days off and that he wasn't leaving my side, but that didn't appease Ollie very much.

It is tough making small talk in a hospital room and I am afraid all three of us fail as masters of the small talk area. After a while, Ollie couldn't get his truck off his mind and the fact that he needed to check on it. He never left it for long and the fact the service center didn't have room to store it inside really bothered him. On top of that, the center wasn't located in the best part of town and all he could imagine was some kids smashing the windows and painting graffiti on it. The worst part was that he wasn't going to be allowed to drive for at least a week at the earliest, so it would just sit at the service center unattended.

Brady said, "Sir, I drove some pretty heavy equipment in the service. If you are comfortable with it, I would be glad to pick it up and drive it to your home."

That was all Ollie needed to know. He started telling Brady all the idiosyncrasies about it and how special this truck was to him. I couldn't believe that he would allow anyone to touch it, but Brady must have engendered some kind of male bonding.

I gave Brady my set of car keys and he drove us to the service center. The plan was that once we picked up the truck, he was going to follow me in the truck back to my home and we'd spend the night there. We didn't have any difficulty picking up the truck from the service center. It took Brady only a few minutes to be comfortable with the multi-gear shifting and then he was ready to go.

It was past dusk as I pulled in the driveway of my darkened house. I was a few seconds ahead of Brady and punched the button to open the garage door. Just as I was ready to enter the garage, a man came running up to my car with a gun in his hand. I swerved the car in his direction and seemed to knock him back. The car continued forward and slammed into the front side of the garage, where it came to a sudden stop. I opened the door, all the while looking to see if I could find the man. When I didn't see him I took off running down the drive just as Brady was pulling in. I probably broke an Olympic record as I scrambled into the passenger's side of the truck.

I told Brady, "There is a man with a gun by the garage."

His first reaction was to draw his gun and go after the

person. I pleaded with him to back up and get out here as fast as he could—and thankfully he listened to me. I grabbed my cell phone and dialed 911, which was beginning to sound like a familiar scenario. I told the operator my name and address and then told her about the gunman. I said, "Check with Detective Miller of the Wood County Sheriff's Department—he knows all about it."

Brady pushed the speed limit for probably a half an hour, and then when he knew no one was behind he pulled into a truck stop and parked among several trucks. It was about as good of a camouflage as we were going to get. At this point I didn't know whom to trust. Could I risk calling Sue again? It was obvious Sue's father hadn't been any help in stopping the attempts on her or my life. I also didn't know if Rev. Rob was responsible for sending a gun man after me. All I knew was that all this drama started after I found out about my bio-father. I needed some time to think, and pleaded with Brady to stay put for the night.

As we were sitting in the truck my cell phone rang, and it was Detective Miller. He told me that he was just about ready to leave my house and that by the time the patrol arrived the gunman was gone. He said that my car was still running when he arrived, so he backed it up and shut it off. The garage door could close, so he did that after using the house key on my ring to have the police officers do a thorough check of the house. I asked him to leave the keys on the kitchen table and I would pick them up later. I thanked him for everything and told him we were spending the night at a truck stop miles from my home. Finally, I said that I would let him know where we ended up staying.

Brady ran to the convenience store at the truck stop and bought some packaged food, soft drinks, and even Polish sausage in a roll. It was apparent that he could eat no matter what was going on. I on the other hand had no appetite, but I did manage to drink a diet soda. After we ate I climbed on the bed and Brady joined me. On a couple of occasions, I had gone with my father on a trip and was use to the truck. When I went with him he set up the pull-down bunk above his bed, but most times when he was alone he just used that space for extra storage. I could tell that this trip in the truck would be totally different from anything I experienced with my father.

Brady was stretched out with only a tee shirt and underwear on. He slapped the bed and said, "We had better get some sleep." He suggested that tomorrow we drive back to Michigan and get some answers from Sue, Edward and Rev. Rob. At first we both lay on the bed trying not to touch one another. After a few minutes I felt Brady's hand on my hip. I didn't think much of it, but slowly our bodies came together and soon we were spooning. His hand moved from my hip to under my top and was gently rubbing my belly. I am sure I moved things along when I groaned and wiggled my butt back into him.

I could feel him harden against my butt cheek and knew he didn't have sleep on his mind. All the while my panties were getting wetter and wetter. Brady's hand started rubbing in bigger circles and were soon at the bottom of my bra. It didn't take long before the hand slipped under the bra and gently rubbed my hardened nipple. I flipped around so that I could face him and when our lips touched my whole body was transcended to another place.

I was pulling his shirt up as he was lifting mine, but the effort was no way fast enough. We both stopped and proceeded to rid ourselves of our clothes. Within seconds we were both naked and totally wrapped up in the sensual pleasure of stroking each other's bodies. He began kissing me and moved down my body. When he reached my breasts his kisses lingered and my nipples puckered to his touch. All the while I was getting hotter and hotter. He wasn't acting fast enough for me and I told him that I really wanted to feel him inside me. I asked him if he had a condom.

Brady was quiet for a moment and then said, "Delta, I'm really sorry, but I don't have anything with me. I stopped carrying a condom in my wallet in high school. I guess I thought that when you and I were ready to make love I would be prepared for it. I just didn't know this was going to happen today, sorry."

The fact that he wasn't always carrying protection told me that he wasn't always looking to get lucky. I looked at him and said, "You have nothing to be sorry about." With that statement I pushed him on his back and started kissing his neck as I slowly moved down his body taking all the time I wanted to enjoy the taste of his body. All the while I was softly stroking him with my hand and enjoying how hard he was becoming. By the time I was finished with him he was like a rag doll.

After a few seconds I said, "See, I said you don't have anything to be sorry about. Are you still feeling sorry?"

Brady came to life immediately and flipped me on my back. He moaned, "I've always believed that turnaround is fair play." I have to say he made me forget about my troubles. My whole body was tingling with pleasure and his tongue was the magic wand. Within minutes he brought me to multiple orgasms. Then he moved back up the bed and nuzzled my neck while saying, "Next time I promise I'll be prepared."

The rest of the night I spent in his arms. Sleep came quickly and the sense of security I felt knowing that he was lying beside me made it very restful. The sound of movement outside woke both of us. The drone of the diesel engines running most of the night was familiar, but now the sound was different caused by the changing gears of the trucks as they were pulling away. We both decided that since we were pseudo truckers we would take advantage of the facilities. Brady bought toothbrushes, toothpaste, shampoo, and soap for each of us. Then for a small fee we were able to use the trucker's showers. Within twenty minutes we both felt like new people.

While eating a trucker's breakfast at the truck stop we had a chance to think through the events of the last couple of days. Brady's police training must have gone into high gear, because he was able to focus on facts not emotions even when we talked about his brother's wife. It was clear that someone was trying to kill me, and it started after Sue talked with her father. Prior to that time, I had spent hours with Sue and there had been no threats on my life. When all was said and done I came to the realization that I trusted Sue and Tom Blakely, but I didn't trust Sue's father and had no reason to trust Rev. Rob.

Brady said, "I think the best plan for us is to drive directly to Tom and Sue's house and not go back to your house. Whoever is out to get you will be watching that house. We have to find out what Sue knows and from that point we can develop our strategy." I didn't have a better plan and told him we should get to Sue's house as soon as possible.

I called Sue to let her know we were coming, and we both decided to hold off talking until I got to her house. Pulling a semi-tractor into a driveway of a family home in an upper middle-class subdivision was not commonplace in her neighborhood. Kids came out of the woodwork to see what was going on. Peter and Alison were just like the rest of the kids, and when they pleaded with Uncle Brady he couldn't resist lifting them into the cab so they could see what it was like in a big rig.

When I entered her house I saw Rev. Rob, the man I had watched on TV for years, standing in the foyer. My emotions were mixed because he was a stranger to me, yet there was something so familiar about him. He walked over to me and said, "Delta, I am Rob Strong and after looking at all the information Sue provided me, I can also say I am your biological father." He then directed my attention to three people standing behind him and said, "I would like to introduce you to my wife Michele and my other children Melissa and Adam." We stared at each other and all were speechless.

Michele was the first to speak. She said, "Rob and Sue have told us everything and we want you to know that we are very concerned about the people trying to do you harm, but very happy to meet you. You have to believe me when I tell you I was shocked, but I trust God has a plan for us and will give us direction."

At that point Melissa stepped forward with her hand out and if I could have gone back in time six years I would have been looking at myself. The five of us were obviously uncomfortable and trying to make the best of the situation. Rev. Rob then said that there was someone else eager to meet me in the living room.

When I went into the living room there was my father sitting on the sofa with Ruby in his lap. He looked tired but seemed to be doing okay. I burst into tears and ran to him. "Dad, is it okay for you to be up? You're not going to hurt yourself, are you?" He pulled me into his arms and said, "Everything is all right now". Tears were running down both our cheeks and it took a few minutes for me to regain my composure.

Meeting my birth father and siblings for the first time made me really uncomfortable. I could only think they were looking at me as if I were a freak that had ruined their lives. Sue tried to create a more comfortable situation by making a pot of coffee and putting out milk and cookies too. I was surprised that the Strong's looked relatively comfortable—at least more comfortable than me. My half siblings broke the ice by talking about school and I learned they were sixteen and fourteen years of age. I wondered if Rev. Rob was dating his future wife at the time he impregnated my mother. After all there were only six years between Melissa and me. I did learn that Melissa was very interested in becoming a doctor too. Adam, on the other hand, was really into hockey and played for a AA bantam team in Ann Arbor.

Sue played the matchmaker with us and was filling in all the pieces that were important to keep us all on the same page. She said that once Uncle Rob had read the information a dim memory came back of a time in the frat house when he drank too much and lost control. He agreed that I was his biological child and he needed time to think about his next steps.

His first and most difficult task was telling his wife Michele and the children about me. Michele was shocked at first but it surprised everyone how fast she came around. It was Michele that reached out to Ollie and arranged for him to be released from the hospital so that he could be with us when I met Rev. Rob for the first time. She also planned to have Ollie stay at their house tonight before returning to our home. Sue said Michele just knew that I would want to have my father close by during this day. In that moment I learned something about Michele's depth of character. The shifting among possessives was amazing—your father, their father, my father, his children, our children…and I didn't what to call Michele other than amazing.

Rev. Rob's presence was powerful. Whenever he talked, everyone else became quiet. He had the respect of his family and in person he was like the man I used to watch on TV. He said, "If you will excuse Michele and me, we have an appointment this afternoon with the media to address the changes in our family constellation. Sue, would it be all right for Mr. Jordan, Adam, and Melissa to stay here? I don't think the kids would like to be part of what has to be done today. We'll pick everyone up before supper."

Sue responded promptly, "Uncle Rob, the kids are always welcome here after all they are my cousins. In fact, when you get back we will have a big family cook-out. Tom loves firing up the grill."

Of course, as soon as they were out the door Sue was creating a shopping list for Tom. When she shouted out to the kids, "What do you want for supper, chicken or hamburgers?" they all yelled "Hamburgers!" She told him to get some brats too, since some of the adults might prefer them to hamburgers. The list got longer and longer as she added rolls, potato salad, cold slaw, chips, some kind of vegetable, beer, soft drinks, and ice cream. Tom seemed happy to get out of the house and said he was off to Trader Joe's, at which time Brady decided to join him.

At 5:00 Sue turned on the TV and we all gathered around to watch it. Sure enough, the newscaster started by saying, "There is going to a special announcement from senatorial candidate Rob Strong that all major networks are simulcasting." Pretty soon there was a picture on the screen of Rev. Rob sanding at a podium with Michele by his side. He started out by thanking the television and news media for giving him this time to speak. After very little small talk, he started talking about family values and how important they were to him.

Rev. Rob said, "For years you have been listening to me tell you about leading a life based on family values. I have always emphasized that family values are more than a single issue such as right to life. Family values encompass a wide variety of actions that are reflected in the way we live our lives. I'm talking about Love and respect, communication, being empathetic, sharing your gifts and riches, tolerance, honesty, forgiveness, and hard work. I never knew that I or my family would be called on to demonstrate those values in a very public manner, but today I am going to do just that.

"I belonged to a fraternity when I was in college twenty-three years ago. Fraternities can be wonderful institutions but they can also be problematic. My fraternity was known as party central. There was always a keg in the game room and every weekend the house was filled with a wide variety of young adults—some students and some not. The fraternity also had special parties for members only, and at those parties, girls from an escort services were hired to entertain and serve us. I am not going to go into the specifics about those parties except to say as a 22-year-old senior I got very drunk at one of the parties. I remember enough to know that I participated in a sexual act with one of the escorts. I never knew her name and she didn't know mine, but it didn't matter since I never head of her again."

"Moving forward to today I am here to tell you that through my actions twenty-three years ago I fathered a child with the woman. For some reason the woman never contacted the university, fraternity, or me. It was only through the miracle of modern science and DNA testing that just this week I learned about my daughter. Was I surprised to learn I had another child? Heck yes! Would I wish that I didn't know of her existence? No! I believe all life is precious, and I believe this young woman is a gift to me and my family. As soon as I knew about my daughter I talked with Michele and the children. They were surprised—or maybe a better word is shocked. However, they are true examples of living their family values and all three took me in their arms not only to forgive me but to love me. They have offered the same expression of love to my newly found daughter. You may be thinking everything I just shared was the reason for this special announcement, but you would be wrong.

"I am standing before you today for one reason. Someone thinking they were helping my campaign hired a man to kill the young woman just identified as my daughter and dispose of her body. There have been two attempts on her life in the last few days, both of which failed, although on both occasions innocent bystanders were injured. The person that contracted with the hit man has shared his remorse for that decision with me and through him I learned that this hired killer will not stop till the job is complete. The person that hired him no longer has a way of communicating that he no longer wants the girl killed. You all know that what this person did supposedly on my behalf is a criminal act and I have contacted the police about the situation and him. So now I am pleading with the individual hired to kill Ms. Delta Jordan, a recent 22-year-old college graduate, to stop this madness. If you are listening to me now, stop what you are doing. You will not get any additional money from the person that hired you.

"Now I would like to address my supporters. As you are now aware of the issues facing my family, I think that it is only appropriate for me to withdraw as a candidate for the US Senate. I am doing this for the benefit of my family because one of my core family values is that the family comes first. I said earlier that I believed Delta Jordan was a gift to me and my family. I can honestly say that it made me realize my failings and to be more accepting of others who have made mistakes. It made me recognize that I am in need of forgiveness by first Delta, Michele, Melissa, and Adam—and then by all the thousands of people that have been part of my life, either as a minister or a senatorial candidate.

"Again, let me plead to the man contracted to kill Delta Jordan: Please, in the name of God, stop right now. To the media I ask that you get that important message out. Thank you."

Chapter 19

By the time Rev. Rob and Michele returned to Sue's house it was nearly 6:30. They were surprised to find everyone had waited for them and food was ready to be served. The conversation was much more comfortable this time. After everyone filled their plates they all seemed to gravitate to the same location as if there was a need for everyone to be close. Rev. Rob said that they tried to make sure no one from the media followed them so that Sue and her family wouldn't be harassed. He also looked at me and said, "Delta, before we sit down to eat, we would like you call us Rob and Michele. Obviously we wouldn't expect you to call us father or mother. I think it would be the most comfortable way to go."

Adam wasn't shy about asking me questions and I could tell his curiosity was getting the best of him. There was a little comic relief when Peter asked why Adam didn't call me Aunt Delta. Sue jumped in and told him that I was really Adam's sister and I was his cousin, but because she and I were really close in age, it was nice for him to call me Aunt Delta. Both Peter and Alison lost interest in the conversation and started playing a computer game in another room on their handheld devices.

I realized that everyone in the gathering knew my story accept Rob, Michele, Melissa, and Adam. So I could understand their interest in me, but at the same time I wanted to know their stories. I started by saying, "I am going to give you the

Wikipedia version of my life tonight, and if we get to know each other better I will share the more difficult details." I told them about my mother, Holly, and how underprivileged I was till I was fifteen. I shared the fact that I was in foster care a few times and that Holly died from alcohol and drug abuse.

It was at this point that I took Ollie's hand and said, "Because of this man, I have led a very privileged life the past seven years." They got the full story of how I begged him to pretend to be a relative and as a stranger he stepped up and turned my life around. There wasn't a dry eye in the room when I told them about Ollie buying a house for me and how he asked if I wanted to be adopted by him when I was eighteen. I told them about going to U of M in Chemical Engineering and that I was accepted to four medical schools.

Sue jumped in at this point and said, "Tom, Brady, and I were at Delta's graduation and the party afterward. It was then I realized how I loved this girl and was so glad to have her in my life. She hadn't changed her last name when Ollie adopted her and at the party she told him that over the past several weeks she had legally changed her name to match his. We all felt fortunate to have been included in that experience and in her graduation."

Rob looked at Ollie and said, "You are a very special man and I believe God intervened so that you could be in Delta's life."

Quiet, strong Ollie looked a little embarrassed but then said, "I can't say if it was God that put us together, but I do know it is the best thing that ever happened to me."

Rob changed the subject when he asked Sue if she had heard from her father. She told him that she hadn't tried since yesterday. Rob said that he called him several times at his office and at home, but got no answer. He wanted to talk with Edward before the police were called, but that hadn't happened. His greatest hope was that Edward could give him more information about the killer than Sue was able to glean from him.

The evening ended pretty quickly after the intense emotional discussions. The Strong's kept their promise about taking Ollie and Ruby to their house. I felt bad about not being with my father, but also relieved in a way, since he wouldn't be harmed by being near me. I also hadn't much time to think about what Rob did today. The man was leading in the race to become a senator, and gave that all up to protect me. Of course the skeptical side of me thought maybe he recognized that telling his base he had an illegitimate child would kill the campaign anyway. On top of everything else, I still didn't know if I was safe. Did the killer watch TV, and would it even matter to him? I guess if he wasn't going to get the full payment, he would possibly think twice whether he wanted to take a risk trying to kill me.

Brady told me that he would be staying at Sue's tonight because there were no police assigned to watch the house, since they didn't know I was going to be there. He told Sue that he would just stay in the guest room with me and Sue didn't bat an eye. She must have assumed there was some chemistry between the two of us. Sue's only comment was to remind us that Peter's room was next to the guest room. Did she think we were going to have wild, screaming sex—or was that my thought? Whoever had that thought was correct.

Brady was lying in the bed when I came back from the bathroom. As soon as I entered the room he held a packet up in the air and said, "See I told you I would never be with you again without protection. Now you know why I went shopping with Tom."

I could feel my face getting red the minute he held up the package of safes. I climbed into bed with just a tee shirt and panties on and quickly realized that Brady was way ahead of me. He grabbed me and held me close as he whispered that this moment was what he had been thinking about all day.

I don't know how he did it but in seconds my tee shirt was over my head. His hands and lips were everywhere and my body was reacting appropriately. My nipples were so puckered they felt like big raisins and my panties felt damp just from his touch. I always feared that I wouldn't enjoy sex, but those fears were long forgotten. We feasted on each other's body and nothing was off limits. When I couldn't take it any longer I pleaded with him to enter me.

Brady proved to be a very wonderful lover. He was responsive to my needs and yet assertive. We totally enjoyed each other even though I was aware of Peter sleeping in the next room. I think we both got very little sleep. I did notice there were three empty packets on the floor when I awoke the next morning, which could explain the lack of sleep.

When the sun came into the room and woke us up we both lay in bed staring at the ceiling. Finally, Brady said, "Delta, I don't know if I should be saying this so soon in our relationship, but I don't want to be apart from you. Last night was absolutely amazing—and I'm not just talking about sex. I have never felt so close to anyone in my life, and soon you will be moving away. I want to give us a chance to see if what I feel is something real—and by real I mean love. I hope you are feeling the same way."

My heart was thumping when he talked about having loving feelings toward me. I felt really close to Brady, but the last weeks had been crazy and I didn't trust any of my feelings. Finding and meeting my birth father, half-sibs, and cousin had been a load to deal with, and then on top of that I had been the target of a hit man. In some ways I thought Brady was being unfair to discuss feelings of love. I hoped he would be more sensitive about my situation. Whatever answer I gave wouldn't be right. Yes, I thought I was falling in love. Yes, I was going to go to medical school. What answer could I give him and be truthful when I didn't know myself?

I rolled on my side and put my arm over his chest while I talked. "Brady, I have feelings for you that I have never felt before. Could I be in love? Probably, but then I ask the question...should these new feelings steer me away from my lifelong dream? I think we have the start of something special and I do want to see where it goes, but you are going to have to deal with being separated from me. I have to get my medical degree and I want to get it from Johns Hopkins. I guess to be honest I want it all. I want to be a medical researcher with a husband and children, but all in good time. If you can't wait for me then you should think twice about continuing our relationship."

Brady stroked my face and said, "I guess you can't fault a man for trying to keep his girl close by, but you have to believe I can wait for you even if you moved halfway around the globe."

I smiled at him and said, "I promise to visit you often, and you can always come to Baltimore to see me. You have to realize that I will be in medical school taking classes for at least three to four years and I have to complete an internship before I get my doctorate. After which I have to do my residency but the good thing is it will be in my field of study, which is biomedical research. So we will have time to think and plan."

Chapter 20

If the children had any concerns about Brady and me sleeping together, it wasn't obvious. They greeted us in their usual cheerful manner and seemed glad to have Uncle Brady and Aunt Delta in their house. I could tell Brady was a favorite of theirs and they quickly talked him into playing a video game with them. That gave Sue and me a chance to talk for the first time.

Sue told me that she was really concerned that she hadn't been able to contact her parents. I told her if Tom could stay with the kids, I would be happy to go with her to their home or her dad's office. I knew that Brady wouldn't let me go alone, and just assumed he would be accompanying us. Sue surprised me by saying that it was a good idea and it was then that I knew just how worried she was. I think she really was worried about finding them both dead by some kind of murder-suicide scenario.

Fortunately, the media hadn't made the connection between Sue and me, so the neighborhood was pretty peaceful when we left. We couldn't say the same for Rob and Michele's house. The early- morning news showed all kinds of media outside their house and it was even the headlines on the national network news shows. *The Today Show* crew had a great time talking about my grand entrance into Rev. Rob Strong's family, and I cringed when I heard them make jokes about the inept hit man. I also noticed that yourancestor.com was advertising like crazy on every network. I knew that within days I was going to be on the front page of every tabloid. In the meantime, overnight polling showed Rob had gained in popularity, particularly among the undecided and Democrats. He did lose some support from the evangelical right. Maybe he would rethink his decision to withdraw from the race.

Sue, Brady, and I headed to Sue's parents' home, which wasn't far away. As we neared the house Sue commented that it was unusual to have a strange car in the driveway so early in the morning. She rang the bell and could hear someone coming to open the door. Her mother opened the door, and her red eyes were a sure sign that she had been crying. As soon as Sue entered she hugged her and kept saying, "Oh Sue, oh Sue."

Sue started to say something when an unknown man walked toward the door. He stepped behind her mother and rested a hand on her shoulder. It seemed like a very familiar gesture and I could tell that Sue took note of it. Although I had met Ann before, she looked past me with no sign of recognition. She did acknowledge Brady, and it was only after Sue said, "You remember Delta," that Ann even nodded her head in recognition.

Ann then turned to the man and said, "I'd like to introduce you to Rev. Bill Titus. He is minister at the Unitarian Universalist Church that I've been attending the last couple of years. I don't know how I would have gotten through the past two years without the love and support of Bill and the congregation."

She invited us into the living room and it was clear that Rev. Titus was going to be part of the discussion. Ann, in fact, made that definite when she said, "Bill knows everything that has happened and I want him to stay." Sue asked her mother what was going on, and where her father was.

Ann started hesitantly and again Rev. Titus rested his hand on her shoulder again in what could be an assuring way, or possibly a loving way. Ann said, "I knew you had an argument with your father but he wouldn't tell me what it was about although I could have guessed it was about that girl," she said, nodding her head in my direction. "I didn't have a clue until Rob called me yesterday trying to find Edward. Rob told me everything including your father hiring a hit man. I knew your father had been up to something, but I didn't think he could go that far. All he seemed to be worried about was his clients, and not protecting Rob. Anyway he didn't come home last night and when Rob went on TV I knew it was a serious matter. The police were here for a couple of hours last night and after interviewing me they went looking for him. It was at that time that I called Bill because I didn't know what I was going to do and I didn't want to be alone."

Sue seemed surprised and stated, "That was thoughtful of you Rev. Titus, but did you spend the whole night here?"

If either of them were embarrassed, it didn't show, and Rev. Titus immediately responded that it was the least he could after all Ann had done for him when his wife died. His statement put a whole new light on their relationship. Months ago Sue had speculated about her mother spending time with the minister, and now it was pretty certain that they had some kind of emotional relationship and maybe even a physical one. While they were talking, Sue's cell phone rang, and it was Tom telling her that a detective had come by wanting to talk with her and me. Sue told him that we would be home in a while, but first she wanted to go to her father's office.

Sue asked her mother if her father took anything with him when he left. Her mother looked a little chagrinned and said, "In the middle of the night I looked for his travel bag and it was gone. There also seemed to be a few clothing items missing, but I couldn't swear to that."

Sue asked the next logical question. "Mother, what about his passport?"

Ann left and went into a room at the back of the house—most likely it was an office. I heard a file drawer slam and assumed she was looking where they kept their passports. She returned to the living and for the first time displayed angry emotions, saying, "That scumbag has taken his passport."

"Mother," Sue said calmly, "have you checked your savings accounts?"

The severity of the situation hit Ann and she ran back to the office. We all joined her and could see she was on the computer. Ann's fingers clicked on the keys and she was in frenzy. After several minutes she turned to Sue and said, "Our savings is gone and his IRAs have been transferred to an unknown account. I still have some money in my IRA, but basically I'm financially ruined." Ann turned and collapsed in Rev. Titus' arms. He didn't hold back his feelings, as he was trying to comfort her.

Sue had had enough of the soap opera, and didn't try to comfort her mother. She did ask her to get the keys to his office. At first her mother hesitated and then remembered that he had a back-up set of keys in the desk drawer. With the keys in hand, Sue told her mother she would be in touch, and out the door we went. Sue talked very little in the car while driving to his office, but did say, "I should be surprised—but to be honest with you, this is just the kind of thing I knew he was capable of. And I should be shocked by my mother's behavior, but how can I fault her for wanting to have someone love her?"

We followed Sue through the foyer to the door leading to Edward Strong & Associates' offices. As expected the door was locked but with the keys in hand Sue opened the lock and flung open the door. The place was in darkness. When she got to her father's office, it was obvious someone had left in a hurry. It looked like things were grabbed on the run and the drawers were left partway open, with papers scattered over the desk and floor. Angela's desk was in no better shape and Sue noticed the phone was flashing to indicate messages. When she activated the answering feature, it indicated there were forty-seven messages. The first several were similar in nature. An investor called because their account balance was showing zero. They assumed it was a computer glitch and would call back. By the fifteenth call, the messages were panicky and the caller was yelling about needing as explanation.

Sue didn't try to access her father's computers because she

knew what the answer would be. Edward had taken his investors' money and fled the country. Furthermore, she suspected that his assistant Angela was with him. Her father had only one concern, and that was himself. Even when he said he hired the killer to supposedly protect her Uncle Rob, it was to get more money in his coffers.

As we were driving back to Sue's house, I expressed my concern for her and told her I couldn't imagine how she felt. Sue looked at me and said, "Delta, you were born into terrible conditions and your first fifteen years were really bad, but my life hasn't been perfect either. My parents never created a loving family and I can only say that similar to you finding a loving father in Ollie, I found a loving family in the Blakely's. It wasn't till I married Tom that I understood what family love was all about. His parents took me in as if I was their own, and I am a better person because of it."

When we arrived at Sue's house, we needed some time to unwind. Brady and I went to the guest room. Sue was filling Tom in on everything when there was a knock on the door and her mother was standing there. Sue walked with her mother to the patio in the back yard, and we could see they were in a heavy discussion. I don't know if Tom was checking on them, but I looked out the bedroom window every once in a while and could see they were really into it. When you watch a heated discussion from a distance, it is like a tennis match. One person says something with gestures and then the other person responds, matching the gestures. Sue and her mother must have come to some understanding because at the end they were both in tears and hugging each other.

Having young children helps to keep things real, because no matter how crazy our day had been the children still wanted to be fed lunch. I witnessed Ann acting like a grandmother and making lunch for the children. In the meantime, Sue walked outside with Tom and I could see she was filling him in on the discussion she had with her mother. When she came back in Sue told Brady and me that she and her mother had a meeting of the minds and that she learned a lot about both her parents that she never knew.

About midafternoon the police returned to question Sue and me but when they learned that Edward's wife was also there, they added her to the list. I really didn't have much to say, since I had met Edward on only one occasion. I did tell them I was shocked that he would hire someone to kill me, because I never considered myself a threat to Rob Strong or to him. I also shared my suspicion that killing me had more to do with Edward's financial dealings than anything else.

Sue had a lot more to talk with the police about. She immediately told them that it appeared her father had left the country and absconded with his clients' money. She described the office and the few messages she had listened to. She also told them about their family savings account being emptied and the passport missing. Finally, she mentioned that her father's assistant, Angela, might be with him. The police reported the information that Sue was sharing to their supervisor. It was easy to see they had all the information they needed from this group, and wanted to obtain search warrants and be on the hunt for Edward.

Chapter 21

Rob called later in the afternoon and asked if I would come to their house. He was direct and upfront with me and said that he wanted to get the media to back off. He felt the best plan was to be a transparent as possible. He believed if the media had all the pictures and stories they wouldn't need to sneak around trying to get candid shots. Maybe he was naïve but it was my kind of thinking too. When I told Brady, he was upset because he thought I would be a better target for the hit man out in the open. He told me that there was no way I could keep him away from attending the media event.

We drove to Rob's house in my father's truck and could see the media still had lots of people there. There were at least four different satellite TV trucks and numerous paper and radio news people. I didn't have Rob's phone number on my cell, so there was no way to warn them that we were close by. Brady blasted the air horn and pulled the truck onto the Strong's' front lawn. I flew out the door and was on the steps in a flash. By the time the media knew what was going on, both of us were in the house.

I immediately ran to Ollie and hugged him. He actually looked pretty good, and if I were to believe him, he was feeling good too. I was surprised that he was as comfortable being in the Strong's' house as he was. I noticed that Adam and Melissa were calling him Ollie, as if they had known him for years.

Ollie even said to me that looking at Melissa reminded him of me when he first saw me walk into that trailer. Likewise, I noticed that Ollie was calling the Strong's by their first names.

Ollie shared with me that they had talked for hours about the situation. He told them lots of details about my schooling and my academic achievements. He talked about our annual vacation to various places, and how it came that we formed such a strong bond. The Strong's apparently were as open with Ollie as he was with them. They talked about their life and also some of the challenges they had. I was feeling a little jealous that I was left out of the talks, because it was clear they had the beginning of a relationship that I didn't have yet.

Rob shared that they all participated in the discussions including Adam and Melissa. They realized that their relationship to Ollie was critical to their relationship with me. Ollie made his view known to me, which was I couldn't pass up the chance to form a relationship with my birth family, but he said that he would support me with whatever decision I made. Rob and Melissa made it clear that they wanted to get to know me. But they especially wanted me to have a relationship with my half-siblings.

Just being with them for a few hours was all it took to prove to me that you can't deny your genes. I could see parts of myself in Rob, Melissa, and Adam. At first I claimed they weren't important to me, but there was something to this birth connection. It wasn't that my love for Ollie would ever change. We were bonded together in a way that nothing could break, but still I was intrigued by my bio family. I could tell

Brady was feeling left out and didn't know how he should respond to me. I couldn't help him at this time because I had enough issues to deal with.

Rob explained his strategy about the media. He described them as hungry birds that would keep pecking away until they got what they needed. He believed if we didn't direct the news, they would create their own stories. By being totally open, they would all have the story they wanted and hopefully move on to the next breaking news. It was determined that we would all go out together as a unit, including Ollie. Only two people would talk to the media, and that was Rob and me. Brady was going to keep an eye on the crowd and look for anyone that was suspicious.

As soon as he took a breath I interrupted and said, "Rob, we have something very serious that may come up and I don't think you are aware of it yet?" When he nodded to continue I said, "Sue, Brady and I visited Edward's office today. It was empty and someone had been going through things in a hurry. There were over forty phone messages from clients all claiming that their accounts had a zero balance. Sue, being a finance person, did a little checking, but basically thought he had stolen his clients' money. On top of that it appears that he has left the country with his assistant. Sue has already notified the police, so we have to assume the press knows about it."

Rob looked as if he had been slugged in the stomach. At first I thought he was going to throw up, but after a few minutes he steadied himself and regained his composure. He couldn't believe his brother could do such a terrible thing. He said, "Okay, if that question comes up I will answer it and I can honestly say it is a police matter and I know nothing about it. If they think we are hiding some information, they may try to connect me to the money, so we have to be totally open with them."

At 4:00 we stepped outside to a temporary podium already loaded with microphones. Rob, being the most comfortable with crowds, stepped forward and got the attention of the group which was no small task. The cameras were on and we could hear the clicking as still shots were taken. Rob explained the ground rules, which were pretty simple. First, he and I would each make a statement and then we would answer questions. If the questions became inappropriate we would not answer them, and if they continued to be inappropriate we would end the press conference.

Rob started by saying the hired hit man was still on the loose and he asked for their help in getting the message to this killer to stop what he is doing. He then introduced all of us starting with Michele, Melissa and Adam. He skipped over me and introduced Oliver Jordan as the adoptive father of his biological daughter. Finally, he introduced me and the news people couldn't contain themselves. They were shouting questions and shooting pictures as fast as they could take them. Rob brought them back under control and gave his brief statement.

Some of his statement was a repeat of the previous day when he talked about the fraternity and his responsibility in getting the escort pregnant. He told them that the first he heard of my existence was a week ago when his niece informed him she had done a DNA search through yourancestor.com and this search uncovered her first cousin. That first cousin happened to be his daughter. At the same time, he learned that his brother had hired a hit man to eliminate his newly found birth daughter, supposedly to protect him. He said that he had had no communication with his brother and that he contacted the police immediately when he learned of the hit man.

Rob stepped back and called me to the microphone. I said that my mother never told me anything about my father and I assumed she was too embarrassed to tell me. I now had to assume that she didn't know who the father was. Oliver Jordan became my guardian when my mother died and he legally adopted me when I graduated from high school. He was the most important person in my life and because of him I had the chance to attend the University of Michigan and would be attending medical school at Johns Hopkins University in Baltimore. I told the group that my father gave me the DNA test as a birthday gift and I never thought it was for real.

I shared how I was surprised when my cousin contacted me as a result of the DNA testing. "We have since become very close and I feel nothing but love for this woman. At the same time, my heart breaks for her because her father did such a heinous act when he contracted with a hit man. With respect to Rev. Strong and his family all I can say is that we are in the beginning phase of building a relationship. We all have agreed that we would like to get to know each other better. You can imagine the emotional issues we are dealing with and we expect our relationship will build over time. I don't know anything about the hit man and wish he would stop. His failed attempts on my life have physically hurt two people I love and it has to stop."

The questions started and they went back and forth between Rob and me. Many of the questions verged on voyeurism. They wanted to know details about my mother and Rob that were not important other than to satisfy the public's prurient curiosity. I felt pretty comfortable talking about my mother's alcoholism and drug addiction and shared that that was why I wanted to get into medical research. I didn't feel comfortable talking about foster care, but fortunately only one person asked me about it. One of the irritating questions I took was from a TV station news caster that asked if we should call him "The Bumbling Hit Man" instead of "The Inept Hit Man." I glared at him and told him in no uncertain terms that the man should not have the notoriety of a nickname, because he was a killer and nearly stabbed my father to death.

Rob jumped in to prevent me from going after the guy. Rob was also giving them all the time they needed to ask questions. Many of the questions were specific to Rob's senatorial campaign and several were regarding his wife and children, excluding me. We thought we were almost done when a reporter from the Detroit Free Press asked what he thought about his brother Edward committing fraud and stealing the life savings of many people. Obviously the other media people didn't know about this, because they all looked at the reporter and backed away. It was almost the way a crowd at a golf tournament back away to form a v shape giving the golfer a clear shot at the hole. In this case it was to give the reporter a clear shot at Rob.

Rob looked at the reporter and said just what he talked about prior to the meeting. "I can honestly say what you are talking about is a police matter and I know nothing about it." The feeding frenzy was on and all the reporters were firing questions. At that time, Rob knew his strategy was no longer effective. In a way I felt sorry for Rob, but it was because of his brother that I had some crazed hit man trying to take me out. Rob then stated that the press conference was over and turned away from the mic.

The atmosphere inside the Strong's' house was one of doom and gloom. Rob wasn't talking and I could tell that he was really hurting over his brother's actions. He excused himself to call Ann, his sister-in-law, and for the first time since the press conference I saw the old Rev. Rob coming back. He was thinking about how much Ann, Sue, and Todd were hurting and he wanted to comfort them. He didn't say what they talked about but I had to believe that he was offering support to Ann. In spite of everything I was impressed with his faithfulness and even though I wasn't a believer, I thought he walked the walk of a "real Christian."

We all watched the local and national news and sat in amazement as the lead story on both the local and national news was us. Some of the side interviews about me were by people I hardly knew such as a 10th-grade history teacher. Rob with all his notoriety got the worst of it. Every well know religious leader and politician seemed to have something to say. Probably the worst parts were the jokes the newscasters were making about the hit man. It seemed every network thought it would be entertaining to call him the "Near Hit Man" or

"Almost Hit Man." They made several jokes about him and didn't continue with our plea to have him stop trying to kill me.

Sue called us in the early evening and Rob put her on the speaker phone so we all could hear what she was saying. She told us she and her mother had been in contact with the detective investigating her father. He told them that a Mr. Edward Strong and Miss Angela Morales had booked passage on a direct flight from Detroit to Madrid, Spain and from there they flew to Andorra. He informed them that Andorra is a small principality in the Pyrenees that does not have an extradition agreement with the United States. Apparently for someone with money it is a good place to hide out.

He also told them that the fraud case had been turned over to the SEC in other words the Security Exchange Commission. The Feds would be looking into his financial activities and although Edward probably stole millions it was still small potatoes to Bernard Madoff's $64 billion thefts. What it meant to Edward's family was that he was classified as a major crook, and the spillover to Rob was inevitable. I also thought about Sue, who wanted to return to the financial industry after her children were older and knew her chances were now little to nil.

I was feeling guilty, because none of this would have come to light if I hadn't taken the DNA test. When I was feeling the worst, I left the room and went to the back patio. In seconds Rob came out and sat next to me. He asked me, "What do you think is happening, Delta?"

I told him just how I felt and that I had destroyed not only his family but also Sue's. He didn't touch me, which in a way I thought he was going to do. Instead he got down on a knee in front of me and looked me in the eye. He said, "I know it is difficult for you to believe, but you coming into my family has been a blessing. I was totally honest when I announced that I was withdrawing from the senatorial race because my family is more important. I don't expect to become your father. As far as I can tell, you lucked out with one of the best fathers a girl could have in Oliver, but I do want to be a part of your life. More important, I want you to be part of your brother and sister's lives. I've only had a short phone call with my mother and she is still trying to understand the situation. I am sure she has seen the news and pictures of you. Delta, you have a grandmother that never knew you existed and I hope you are open to meeting her too."

"I don't know why Edward did what he did. He knows well enough that I would have given up politics in a minute for my family. Edward was always about the money, and he and I are quite different. The decisions he made were his choice, and you did not ruin Sue's life. If anyone caused Sue grief, it was Edward. Furthermore, I think I know Sue pretty well, and I believe if it meant losing her father or losing you, she would choose to keep you."

Rob continued,"The most important thing we can do now is keep you safe. We don't know if this mad man heard our plea, but we can be extra cautious. Brady and I were talking and he has asked for personal leave from the Plymouth Police Department so that he can provide protection. We also have contacted the Wood County Sheriff's Department and told them that you and Oliver will be returning home tonight. Your secluded environment may be an easier place to protect you. Outside of that, all we can do is pray that the killer watched the news."

Chapter 22

Everyone gathered in the Strong's' living room and it was decided that Ollie, Brady and I would return to Greenville. This would get me out of the eye of the press and it would be easier for Brady to know if a stranger was lurking around her house in the country. Rob was going to try to contact his brother and hopefully get more information about the hit man. He knew that Edward's bad decisions were his own, but he still couldn't help but feel responsible for the crimes that his brother committed. If he wasn't running for office, his brother might never have concocted the scheme to defraud his clients or hire a hit man.

The next step Rob took was contacting Edward's family. He called Ann, Sue, and Todd and arranged to meet with them at his attorney's office. Until he had the chance to sit down with them as a group, he wouldn't know just how damaging Edward's crimes were to the family. There was no doubt in his mind that they needed legal counsel, particularly when the lawsuits against Edward started coming. After Rob completed the calls to his extended family, he was ready to go.

The plan was for Brady and me to drive my father's rig, because Ollie wasn't in any shape to drive. Then Rob would drive Ollie to my home. The problem was that the media were still camped in the front of the house. A call to Sue helped solve this little dilemma. Brady went to the truck alone and started it up. The press didn't know who he was and so they weren't interested in him. Rob arranged for the remaining three of us to cut through his neighbor's back yard so that we would end up on another street. Within a few minutes we heard the sound of a diesel and saw the big green tractor come around the corner. Right behind Brady were Tom and Sue each driving separate cars. After a quick hug, Sue tossed her keys to her Uncle Rob and she jumped into Tom's car.

Before we even got started, Rob yelled that he had to stop for gas and told us to go on ahead. During the drive, Brady and I tried to problem-solve the situation but we got stymied by the idea of protecting ourselves from an unknown hit man contracted to kill me. The fact that we didn't know if the hit man paid any attention to the television reports kind of paralyzed us. I tried to be optimistic, but that didn't work. The DNA test that put my life at risk had also brought me so many good things. I wouldn't have Brady in my life or know my birth father and siblings. I also had a paternal grandmother that I had yet to meet.

The ride was pretty uneventful. There was very little traffic on the road and we made good time going to Greenville. When Brady pulled into the driveway at my house I felt a sense of relief. I was back on familiar ground and maybe everything would be all right. My Jeep was right where I left it and although the house was in darkness, everything looked good. I told Brady to pull the truck onto the extra pad next to the garage that Ollie had put in years ago. He reached over took my hand and said, "Well, you're home, honey. Let's get inside."

Brady opened his door and got out of the truck. I was a little behind because I was picking up my pocketbook. I had just stepped on the ground when I heard a gunshot on the other side of the truck. I yelled for Brady, but didn't hear a thing. With the truck's lights off I couldn't see much of anything, but then I heard a gravelly voice say, "Call me a Near Miss Hit Man—you think you all can make fun of me and get away with it? I'll show 'em who is a near miss hit man. Kiss your sorry ass goodbye."

Just then, Rob turned into the driveway and the car headlights lit up the gunman standing about ten feet from me. He seemed startled and turned toward the car, but didn't shoot. Rob, on the other hand, must have punched the gas pedal to the floor immediately because he drove the car directly into the hit man. I heard the crash of the body against the car and saw the man fly several feet away. Both doors of the car flew open and Ollie was by my side in seconds. Rob stood by his door and looked in shock.

I yelled, "Rob, Brady's been shot and he is on the other side of the truck." My voice brought him out of it and he ran around the truck. By the time Ollie and I got there, Rob was kneeling next to Brady. My first thought was that he was dead, and it was only when I got close to him that I saw his eyes were open, and he asked, "Are you okay?" When Ollie saw that Brady was going to make it, he went in search of the killer. In seconds he yelled back that the hit man wasn't going to hurt anyone again.

I grabbed my cell phone and called 911. It was getting to

be a familiar pattern and I almost expected the 911 operator to answer, "Oh hi Delta, what's happening? Do you need another emergency vehicle out there?" I gave her the basic information and told her that one person was dead. I also suggested that she contact Detective George Miller since he was familiar with the situation.

While we were waiting for the emergency vehicles to arrive I walked over to Rob and asked how he was doing. He looked in shock but managed to say, "I have taken someone's life."

On impulse I threw my arms around him and held him close. It was the first time we had actually touched and both of us were aware of it. He seemed to gain strength by my touch. This man, who had given me life and didn't know it, had without regard to his own personal conscience done something to save my life. In one week my existence had scrambled up his life so bad that it was difficult to see how it could be repaired. However, within a few minutes he again regained his composure as I had seen him do a couple of times in the last few days.

I released him from my grip and he looked at me and said, "Are you okay?"

The EMT, fire department, and police arrived also simultaneously. The EMTs went to work on Brady and I was in a dilemma because they loaded him in the ambulance and I wanted to be with him. Both of my fathers looked at me and together said, "Go, we'll take care of things back here."

Although the wound to Brady's shoulder was not life

threatening, it did significant damage. He was in surgery for a couple of hours and I paced the waiting room floor. Finally, the surgeon came out and talked to me. He didn't have much personality and sounded more like an anatomy professor. He said, "The anatomical structure of shoulder is such that there are bones, joints, muscles, soft tissues, blood vessels, and nerves all surrounded in a comparatively narrow region. Any injury to the area can cause damage to these structures, and consequences may vary depending on the part injured. The shoulder joint has many structures involved, and gunshot wounds can cause varying degrees of injury."

"The biggest concern with Brady's injury was to the shoulder joint. The gunshot wound occurred in the area that affects the articulation of the shoulder joint, and meticulous evaluation was necessary to rule out the presence of bullet fragments in the area. I had to remove the fragments and rebuild part of the joint. It will be a slow recovery, but with physical therapy he should get back to almost 100%. I understand he is a police officer, and if he is lucky he will be able to return to duty, but when that will happen remains to be seen."

Just after the doctor left, both Ollie and Rob came into the waiting room. They said the police had interviewed both of them and would talk with me tomorrow. They didn't know the name of the hit man, but it was clear he had a vendetta against me. Both of my fathers talked about how fearful they were for my life when they saw the man pointing a gun toward me. It was clear that my life would never be the same and I only hoped that it wouldn't be worse. Things had been going so well for me and I thought I knew where I was going. Now, I had a quasi-boyfriend, a birth father, and two half-siblings whom I really didn't know, just at the time I was moving 700 miles away. The one thing I knew was that I had a first cousin that I now knew and loved. Wow, talk about life-altering events.

I had fallen asleep with my head on Brady's bed when I felt a hand on my head. I opened my eyes and saw Brady looking at me. His right arm and shoulder were totally bandaged but his left arm was free and his hand had found its way to my head. "How are you feeling?" I asked.

"I don't remember much other than getting out of the truck. What happened to me?" he asked.

"The hit man shot you as soon as you stepped off the truck and onto the ground. I couldn't see you and didn't know what happened, but then he came around the other side to shoot me. The whole time he was ranting about being made a fool of and made some statement about the national news calling him a Near Miss Hit Man. Just when he was ready to shoot me, Rob and my father drove into the driveway. When the car's headlights illuminated the killer, he froze just long enough for Rob to speed up and hit him with the car. He didn't survive, and thankfully now that I know you are going to make it, everything else is going to be okay.

"All I keep thinking is if he hadn't paused to complain about being called names, I would be dead. Changing the subject—the doctor said you can make a good recovery but it will take a time before your shoulder fully heals. I probably shouldn't be saying anything and let the doctor tell you," I said.

I spent most of the next two days at the hospital with Brady. During that time, I got to really know his parents and could see why Sue loved them. They were so giving and accepting. As worried as they must have been about Brady, they never once made me feel I was the blame for Brady being shot. In fact, it was just the opposite—they talked about how much Brady had told them about me and how important I was to him. I got the impression that he hadn't talked about any girlfriends before me.

Brady was released from the hospital and after much discussion between Brady, his parents, and me it was decided that he should go to his parents' house for the initial recovery. At first I wanted him to come to my house but had to agree it would be too challenging. I was wrapped up in the police investigation and had appointments with the Wood County authorities and with the Northville Police, since they still had it as an open case.

Rob didn't have an easy out for the situation. The police had to do a thorough investigation but the well-documented history paid off. It took a couple of weeks before the prosecuting attorney determined that he wasn't going to file charges. I am sure he was concerned that his decision would be examined under a microscope and he wanted all of the i's dotted and t's crossed.

When I visited the Northville Police, I stayed with Sue. Her family was still reeling over her father's actions. He might be safe from extradition in Andorra, but he would never be able to return to the United States without being arrested. He would never see his children and grandchildren again. In reality, he was the real loser. The financial fraud case made all the news channels and the sad truth was that he stole the retirement and safety net from many people. Sue told me he sent a letter to her and Todd apologizing to his family, but in the letter he tried to justify his actions by saying it was the only way he could get out of some bad investment decisions. He didn't send a letter to her mother, and she was as much a victim as his clients.

I had about four weeks before heading to Baltimore for medical school. I spread the time between Ollie, Brady, Sue's family, and Rob's family. I didn't know how my relationship with my birth father would develop. I had a great deal of respect for him, but it wasn't love—at least not now. Adam and Melissa were able to visit me at my house in Greenville, and that was the really a nice time. I could see us start to form a bond and they clearly felt some kind of bond with Ollie.

It was not going to be easy to continue the relationship with my birth family, particularly with me moving. It was something that we all would have to consciously work at. One piece that was critical in this situation was how supportive Michele, Rob's wife, was to everyone. If she had been against our forming a positive relationship, it would have been nearly impossible. She had a lot to lose by my entrance into the family, and yet became the real stabilizing force.

I had been getting calls from book publishers, ghost writers, and every talk show host on the major television networks, Netflix, HBO, and several movie studios. I never returned a call and couldn't imagine dealing with them. One day I received a call from Rob and he asked to meet with me at his office. I had no idea what he wanted to talk about, but with our relationship so new I was hesitant to question his request. So we agreed on a day and time.

His office was in a nondescript office building in a Detroit suburb. Since leaving the church he had used the office to prepare for his speaking engagements, television appearances and book writing. I had no difficulty finding the building and his office was clearly marked. There was a reception area with a person I assumed to be his secretary sitting at the desk. She must have assumed who I was or seen my picture on TV because she immediately said, "Ms. Jordan, Reverend Strong is expecting you. Please enter. Can I get you anything—coffee, tea, water?" I told her I was fine and entered the office.

In looking at his office the old saying came to mind, "A clean desk is the sign of a sick mind." There were stacks of papers and books all over his desk and counter work space. Rob was sitting behind a large mahogany desk and sitting in front of it was a man I had never seen before. Rob immediately came around the desk and gave me a hug. He then turned to the other man and said, "Harless, I'd like you to meet my daughter Delta Jordan. Delta, this is Harless Burke, an old friend and publisher of several of my books."

My first response was to run from the office. I felt he had brought me there and was going to hit me with this elaborate plan to write a book of our experiences. All I could say was, "How could you?"

Rob wasn't dissuaded by my attitude and calmly said over and over, "Relax, Delta—take a seat and relax." I guess I listened to him because I started to calm down and eventually did sit down.

Rob recognized how tense I was and started out slowly, "Delta, I asked Harless to meet with us today because he is someone that I would trust with my life. I think we both need to hear what he has to say before we go off in different directions. I called Harless because I have been hounded by writers, producers, and studios. I think you probably have more of that type after you than were after me. Harless has done some ground work that could be helpful."

Harless spoke in a baritone voice with a slight New York accent. "You and Rev. Strong are the hottest prospects the entertainment field has seen in a long time. I am not making light of your situation but books, movies, and TV are in the entertainment field. When Rob called me, I did a little searching and was shocked at the numbers these companies were throwing around. Rob asked for my opinion and I told him which company to go with. This movie studio wants the rights to your book and movie and are willing to pay in the high seven figures for it."

I was shocked and dismayed that Rob would go ahead and cut a deal after all we had been through. I looked at him and said, "I am so disappointed in you. You talk about family values and love and yet you sold out to the highest bidder. All the years I watched you on TV I thought to myself that this is a man whose standards are unwavering. What right do you have to sell my story? All you did was donate your sperm and then didn't even remember donating it." I fumed on for several minutes until I ran out of steam.

Harless spoke again. "Delta, you've misunderstood me. Rob wasn't trying to sell your story, at least not for himself. I better let him explain."

Rob took a deep breath and released it slowly. Then he looked at me and said, "Delta, this story is going to be written—if not by you, then by someone that has no connection to us. You have a chance to do something really wonderful and this is what I want to suggest to you. First, I believe it is important to make sure you are secure. Medical students are left with huge debts that often control what they do after graduating. If you can graduate debt free then you can decide if you want to work for a small research company and or do research on your own. You won't need to earn the big bucks to pay off student loans. The average medical student has a student loan debt close to $200,000. Think of what it would mean to have no debt.

"The second piece of the puzzle that has been bothering me, and I know it has been bothering Sue and Todd, is the pain and suffering caused by their father's actions. I am suggesting that after your needs are met the rest of the money goes into a fund to assist those families hurt by Edward. Obviously, they wouldn't get all their money back, but it could help a little.

"The third piece of the puzzle is that we would pre-empt all of the money-hungry bastards that are looking out for themselves. A story in your words and with my part connected will be the biggest attraction. I also hope you realize that I do not want any money from this venture."

I was a little chagrined by my previous behavior, and all I could do was look at my birth father with admiration. Rob hadn't thought about himself and was trying to work something out that would benefit many people. Somehow I had the wherewithal to say that I needed time to think and I also had to talk with my father before any decision would be made. I did have one suggestion for him to think about. I thought that the fund to help the people defrauded could be managed by Sue. This would allow Sue to feel as if she were doing something positive and to also utilize her skills in the best way.

Rob smiled and said, "I like your thinking."

I drove home to Greenville after the meeting and was so grateful to find Ollie down in his workshop. His chest wound was almost healed and he probably was ready to return to work. When I looked around the shop, I noticed a number of new pieces I hadn't seen before. His woodworking skills were getting better and better. He smiled as I came down the basement stairs and welcomed me home. There was something so serene about the atmosphere—I didn't want it to end.

Over dinner I told Ollie everything that had happened. As usual, he listened without interrupting me—and it is amazing how few people allow that to happen. Most people interrupt a speaker continually asking for clarification and sharing something in their own life that came to mind. After I unloaded everything I had to say, Ollie looked at me and said, "What do you think you should do?"

"Oh, come on, Dad—this movie or book or whatever is also your life. You have a part in this decision too," I retorted. "I'll tell you what I think, but I want to know your opinion too. At first I was opposed to any consideration of a book or movie. Then I accepted the notion that if I didn't take charge, someone else was going to write about my life. I must also admit that getting through medical school without any debt is appealing. I wasn't so sure about trying to assist the people that invested with Edward. I thought if they were greedy enough to invest with a slime bag like Edward, they deserved what they got.

"Then I thought about Sue and how her life has been impacted by the course of events. I don't know her brother Todd, but I am pretty sure he is having a hard time too. I also know that Sue is worried about her mother and I can understand that. So I guess what I am saying is that overall Rob's plan is a good one."

Ollie looked at me and said, "That's what I thought from the moment you mentioned it. I could help you a little with medical school, but there would still be a large debt. There is nothing wrong with looking out for yourself. In fact, if you got the money for medical school, I just might put the truck up for sale and call it quits. I've been putting money away on a regular basis and have enough saved to retire now. In a few years, social security will kick in and that will give me even more. Besides, I have really enjoyed hanging around the house and doing woodwork. I didn't tell you, but I have three pieces in a little decorating shop in downtown Greenville."

I was surprised by his response—not by the part about taking the money for the book and movie rights but by his admitting that he was continuing to drive only to help pay for my college and that he would like to stay around home. I smiled at him and said, "Well, I guess that's that. I'll call Rob in the morning and get the ball rolling."

Chapter 23

The whole book and movie process was much more complex than I imagined. It was getting very close to my time to go to Johns Hopkins when the deal was finally done. It ended up that a large movie studio won the bidding war for the book and movie rights. Both Rob and I had to fly to California to meet with the executives, which also gave us time to continue working on our relationship. Rob's attorney provided legal support all the way through it and made sure that we had a certain amount of control. We came home from California with the contracts and had 48 hours to review and sign them.

I had my own team looking out for me. Sue and Brady were with me the whole way. Brady had only a few classes in law school, but he had a very legalistic mindset. Sue, with her financial background, really understood how to work the numbers. Together they were a terrific team and I felt confident enough to sign the contract after 24 hours. In the contract $600,000 was earmarked for me, which I felt guilty about. Sue and Brady worked me over on this point and convinced me that without me there would be no story.

The hardest task for Rob and me was convincing Sue to become financial manager of the foundation that yet was to be established. The language in the contract allowed us to form a nonprofit foundation with the purpose of assisting victims of financial fraud. We stayed away from dealing specifically with the crime that Edward Strong committed. Rob was having his attorney complete the legal work necessary to establish the foundation.

The more I thought about my situation, the more I supported the idea of using the resources I now had available to help others. How often does someone have the opportunity to help others in a really significant way? On top of that, I would be foolish to reject money that could fund my medical education. If I didn't use money from the book and movie sales, Ollie would be trying to pay for my education, and that wasn't fair to him.

What I didn't expect was the announcement that the movie studio prepared for our signing of a contract. The week before I was supposed to leave for Johns Hopkins they had me booked on the *Today Show*, *Good Morning America*, and *Morning Joe*. The studio was trying to whet the public's appetite, but I thought the interviews were more salacious than anything else. The general public seemed to focus more on the circumstances of my mother's impregnation then on any other aspect of my life.

I guess I was being Pollyannaish about the whole thing and thought they should be focusing on someone succeeding when all odds were against them. I actually thought that my life was a tribute to the love and support of an adoptive father and the undying effort on my part to achieve success against terrible odds. In most interviews, it got back to questions about my mother being a prostitute, and Rob's behavior as a college student.

I have to admit that many people were intrigued by the DNA testing and all the major ancestry companies wanted me as a spokesperson. I am sure that I am only the tip of an iceberg, and that over the next few years, hundreds or thousands of people will be connected with birth family through DNA testing. Am I glad I did it? I don't know. I was very happy and content before I did the DNA testing. I was never concerned about my paternal parentage. Maybe once I was married and bearing children, my position on that matter would change, but honestly I was happy with Ollie as my father and not knowing any other relatives.

The positive thing to come out of this situation is meeting my cousin and of course my half-sibs. I couldn't deny the connection that one feels to their blood relatives. In reality I fantasized that my blood relatives would be with me forever, regardless of what happened. I knew that wasn't the case, but that's what I thought.

Rob and his family seemed to be handling things fairly well. My half-sibs were pretty together kids and I could envision having a great relationship with them in the future. Just the thought that my children would have an aunt and uncle made me feel warm inside. Michele was a very neat person and I could see that she wielded a lot more influence in the family than one would have guessed. Throughout this whole crazy event, she was the rock, and I will be forever grateful to her.

Rob, my birth father, landed on his feet. The polls showed a surprising amount of support for him, but he stuck to his guns and did not run for the Senate. However, his speaking engagements increased tenfold, and book offers were coming in. His popularity had never been higher. A lot of the surge had to do with his openness in talking about fathering a child that he didn't know about and then his acceptance of that child. This behavior resonated with the public and made him sort of a folk hero.

At the same time, he was going through a metamorphosis in regard to his political and religious views. He was seeing things through a different lens. For example, he always talked about family values in a way that blamed people for not living the way he lived. The experience of having to actually live those values changed him. As he has said on TV many times, "It's easy to tell people what you stand for, but showing people what you stand for through your actions is a much more difficult thing to do." Rob showed us all, and I am a believer in him.

Brady and I had not been able to spend much time together since his being wounded. I have heard from other people that shoulder injuries are some of the worst to recover from and I can see that was the case with Brady. He was going to physical therapy three times a week but barely could lift his arm above up to his shoulder. He was put on short-term disability by the police department, which meant at least six months off work, but I wouldn't be surprised if his recovery was longer.

We tried to see each other as much as possible, but with everything going on, it was a challenge. He spent a couple of days in Greenville and I would do the same at Sue's house. I can honestly say that I have never loved a man like I loved

Brady, but at the same time I was so aware of the upcoming separation. All I could think of was how difficult it would be to maintain a long-distance relationship.

My days of living with Ollie were growing short. We had been together for over seven years and the thought of never living together again as father and daughter was hard for me to take. In reality, I was going through the same feelings of separation that most students go through when they leave home and recognize things will never be the same again—it's just that most students do it early in the college life and here I was starting medical school and just doing it.

Ollie, as usual, made it easy on me. The truck was up for sale and he convinced me that our house would always be there for me whenever I needed to return and he made sure I knew that he expected me back a few times every year. He seemed happier than I had ever seen him. The furniture pieces he was building were extremely impressive and I could envision him having a huge demand for his work. What he didn't know just yet was that I made sure that $300,000 dollars of my contract went to Ollie. It was nowhere near what I owed him, but it was something I could do right now.

My Cherokee was packed and I was eager to go. I stood outside the car hating this moment, but also loving it too. Ollie, Brady, Sue, Tom, Peter, Alison, Rob, Michele, Melissa, and Adam surrounded me. If there was any record for a group hug, we just established it. In less than a year I had gone from one relative in Ollie to ten relatives that all cared for me.

Brady took me in his arms and held me for what seemed

like an eternity. I told him I would be home for Christmas and he made promises to come to Baltimore. Both of us were telling each other things we didn't know would ever happen. I got in the car, started the engine, and pulled out of the driveway. I couldn't see then through the rearview mirror because my eyes were blurry with tears.

Epilogue

It was a beautiful day—almost summerlike for early May in Baltimore. I had picked up my gown and hat and was really ready for this special occasion. Sensing a need for solitude, I drove to the harbor to sit and watch the activity. As I was sitting there I recollected what has happened to my life. It has been an amazing five years and I learned more than I ever thought possible. Johns Hopkins met all my expectations and then some. Tomorrow I would be awarded my Medical Doctorate and would have accomplished a lifelong goal. Today, I would be greeting my family as they arrive from Ohio and Michigan so they can support me during this occasion. I still was amazed to have a family that would travel 700 miles for a graduation but that is what I had. They had all made hotel arrangements at the same place because my apartment was crowded enough.

I had to chuckle to myself how as humans, things we thought were so important might turn out to be so unimportant. I always thought research was going to be my specialty, and I could never have predicted that I would go in a different direction. The tide turned on a cold winter's night at Sinai Hospital in Baltimore where I was doing my rotation in the emergency room. The ambulance delivered a 32-year-old woman who was comatose from suspected drug and alcohol use. Also in the ambulance was a young pre-teen girl who was visibly shaken. I was acutely aware of the young girl, but my attention had to be focused on the mother.

I immediately ordered a tox screen to find out what poison was in her system. This hospital was very familiar with drug overdoses and knew that toxicology is one of the few areas in medicine where 24 hours a day, seven days a week, you have the option to call a friend in the poison center when you have questions. The first few hours are critical to the outcome and recovery of a drug overdose. I had to know if the overdose was activating or deactivating the central nervous system. The toxicologist got back to me quickly and I knew my patient ingested drugs and alcohol that were deactivating the central nervous system. I cautiously recommended some short-acting sedatives and then managed her airway through ventilation. I knew that people in her condition die because they lose their airway. With the combined effort of the staff I knew this woman would recover, but the question in my mind was whether the daughter would recover.

As soon as the patient was stable, I gave the attending nurse instructions and told her I would be in the waiting room. As I entered the waiting room I checked the clock and it was after 3:00 in the morning. I asked the emergency room receptionist where the child was that accompanied the woman in ER Room 3. She said, "The girl gave me all the identifying information, including her mother's medical insurance card. She told me she was eleven, but I thought I was talking with an adult. Anyway she is curled up in the chairs against the wall."

Sure enough, what at first glance looked like a pile of coats was actually the girl lying down across three chairs. I walked over and kneeled on the floor next to her. I gently rubbed her shoulder until she woke up. To me she didn't look like an adult. She was a scared child that had learned to mask her fear—because what other choice did she have? She stared at me with tear-swollen eyes and asked about her mother. She seemed to have resigned herself to hearing bad news and I probably surprised her. Going through my mind was that I had been this little girl seventeen years ago and nobody came forward to help me.

I said, "I am Dr. Jordan and I have been helping your mother. I want you to know that she is resting comfortably and she has responded to the treatment we have provided. What's your name?"

She told her name and before long shared that her mother had just broken up with her boyfriend and was really sad. She also said she had been in foster care one other time and was really scared that she would have to return. I don't know how the other medical staff felt about my actions, but I took the girl in my arms and told her I knew how she was feeling. I wasn't going to tell her everything would be okay, because that would not be the truth. In time she told me she had an aunt and uncle living in Chevy Chase who always called to check on her and her mother. Together we located the uncle and made the middle of the night call that everyone hates to receive. The uncle said he was the mother's brother and that he would be at the hospital in less than two hours.

A couple of days later I received a card from the girl's

uncle and in it was a handwritten letter from the little girl thanking me for helping her when she really needed it and also for saving her mother. The uncle added that he and his wife had temporary custody until such a time, if ever, that her mother is ready to have her back. He added that he never knew of a doctor that would take the time in an emergency situation to help a young child, but he was glad that I had been there for her.

I knew then that I had a calling. I didn't want to be stuck in a lab. There are plenty of scientists that love looking through microscopes, but that isn't me. I felt myself come alive in the emergency room. When people were in the greatest distress was the time that I could really focus my knowledge and skill and make a difference in their lives.

I snapped out of my day dream and realized I had to get ready for the upcoming event. Throughout the afternoon and early evening my relatives were arriving. Since all my guests booked rooms in the same hotel, that made it easy to coordinate things. Ollie drove with Sue, Tom, Peter, and Alison. The others—Rob, Michele, Melissa, and Adam—flew in and rented a car. I greeted them all at the hotel and gave them the itinerary for the next day. I actually had two ceremonies. The first one was the graduation ceremony for Johns Hopkins and that was at 8:30 in the morning on the Homeward Field of the Homeward Campus. It was at this occasion that my name would be announced.

The second event was the School of Medicine Convocation and that was at Joseph Meyerhoff Symphony Hall at 2:30 p.m. So I had marks on a campus map showing the best place to park and had written down all the other details that were needed. Between ceremonies I had arranged for us all to eat together at—where else but Red Lobster. They didn't have a separate room, but they promised me they would put us in a location where we would all be together.

I was surprised that it took so long before the next question was asked, and it was my half-sib Adam that did the asking. He said, "Okay, we didn't come all this way to see you. Where is he?"

I smiled and said, "He's back at the apartment taking a nap with Brady, but if you all can tolerate pizza, we have lots of it for you at my place. Why don't you come to my apartment in an hour and everything will be ready for you."

Brady was eager to see everyone and when the first knock came he was there to open it. Standing at the door was Sue, Tom, and the kids. They forgot about Brady and gravitated toward what he held in his arms. Most of them were meeting our six-month-old son, Oliver, for the first time. Sue flew out when I gave birth to help me out at home for the first week and my father got to the apartment just as I was going into labor. The rest of them were greeting Oliver for the first time.

Sue, Peter, and Alison were related to baby Oliver in a couple of ways. Since I was Sue's 1st cousin, baby Oliver was her 2nd cousin and Peter and Alison were his 3rd cousins. However, since Brady was Tom's brother, that made Tom baby Oliver's uncle and Sue his aunt by marriage and Peter and Alison his 1st cousin. It sounds rather complicated, but it worked. Rob and Michele had no trouble claiming the status of grandparents.

And Melissa and Adam couldn't wait to meet their first nephew. I thought there might be a problem between Rob and Ollie about what they wanted to be called but that situation was resolved pretty easily. My father announced that he wanted to be called Daddy O and Rob said he wanted to be called Grandpa. In the end, everyone seemed quite happy.

Brady was beaming and I could tell he was a real proud papa. When his shoulder didn't heal quickly and still gave him a problem when he reached above his head, he decided to follow his dream and to follow me. He moved to Baltimore at the end of my first year and enrolled in the University of Maryland Francis King Carey School of Law. He actually graduated a year ahead of me because I lost a whole semester with my pregnancy and parental leave.

When everyone had arrived and the time was right I asked for quiet and said, "Brady and I have an announcement to make and no I am not pregnant. What we want to tell you is that Brady has passed the bar in Michigan and has accepted a position as an assistant district attorney for Oakland County and on top of that I will be doing my residency at Henry Ford Medical Center in Detroit. Henry Ford is a special place; it is a nearly thousand-bed medical center with the full complement of residency programs and is in the middle of a major urban city. I feel like this is emergency medicine at its truest form."

I think the whole apartment building could hear the cheers when they realized we were coming home.

Ollie came up behind me and leaned close to my ear to whisper. "This is like a dream come true. You are an MD with a husband and baby. You have a wonderful extended family, but always remember you have someone who will always be in your corner, Me. I love you and you know any time you need someone to look after little Ollie, don't think twice about calling me."

THE END

Acknowledgements

The idea for the novel came from an experience my wife had after completing a DNA test through an ancestry site. What we assumed would be more like an old fashion parlour guessing game actually was much more serious. Shortly after getting the results back from the test she received an email from a person trying to find her birth family. Within minutes she knew that this person's mother was a cousin that had given up a child for adoption 42 years earlier. The idea that through a little bit of saliva the long buried history of your family could be discovered was intriguing and eye opening.

My thanks goes out to those that advised, proof read and supported me in the writing process including, Marcia Downs, Bob Downs, Rick Shrock, Marcia Pyrah, Paige Harding Harris, Gary Harris, Jill Palmer and Ann Fisher. I want to offer a special thank you to Melissa Peterson, Jay Liedman, Diane Liedman and Nancy Goodwin, my wife, for making the DNA world become real for me.

CPSIA information can be obtained at www.ICGtesting.com
Printed in the USA
BVOW08s0849200716

456214BV00027B/14/P